Kate was reaching for the spoon to take some pasta salad when someone else reached for it and bumped her hand.

"Sorry," she said.

"You first," said a guy's voice.

Kate looked over and saw the boy with the golden eyes standing beside her.

"Hi," he said. "I'm Tyler."

"I'm Kate," she said. Then she couldn't think of anything else to say, so she just stood there, feeling stupid.

Just then someone called to Tyler, and he walked away, Kate found herself with all kinds of questions. Who exactly was Tyler? Why was he at the ritual? Was the woman his girlfriend? Why did she care anyway? She had a great boyfriend. She was even wearing the ring he gave her.

Still, as she spooned pasta salad onto her plate, she couldn't stop thinking about the boy with the golden eyes.

Follow the Circle:

book
2

merry meet
isobel bird

AVON BOOKS

An Imprint of HarperCollinsPublishers

merry meet

chapter 1

"I can't believe we're finally here," said Kate Morgan, looking around the room and smiling at the handsome guy seated across from her. Their table was in the corner, next to a window. Outside a fine, gray March mist floated across the pier on which the restaurant was built, but from time to time it parted and Kate could see the reflection of the moon on the ocean. The small candle on the table in front of her flickered cheerfully inside its glass holder and made her forget the chill that had wrapped around the town only a few days before the official start of spring.

"Hey, I told you—I always keep my promises," Scott Coogan said, his lips parting in the carefree smile that was one of the things Kate found so appealing about her boyfriend.

Her boyfriend. The very words sent a tingle of excitement flowing through her skin like electricity. As she looked into Scott's blue eyes, Kate couldn't believe that only six weeks earlier she and

Scott had never even spoken to one another. *If it hadn't been for the spell I cast*, she thought to herself.

The spell. Kate still felt terrible about the spell. When she had found the book of spells in among the other books she'd checked out of the library for her report on the witchcraft persecutions for history class, she'd thought it was all ridiculous. The rituals and chants were fun to read, but she didn't think they would really do anything.

Not until she tried one. The "Come to Me Love Spell" had seemed harmless when she'd read it in the book. It had even seemed harmless when she'd tried using it to get Scott to notice her. And when he *had* noticed her, she was as surprised as anyone else. Surprised and happy. At least until all the bad things started happening afterward.

But she didn't want to think about that anymore. It had been awful. If it hadn't been for Cooper and Annie, she didn't know where she'd be right now. Probably still trying to figure out how to reverse the spell that had gone so out of control. If she could have done it at all.

In the end she and her friends had stopped the spell. And best of all, Scott was still with her, even without the use of magic. Still, sometimes Kate found herself wondering if he *really* liked her or if he was still a little bit enchanted by the ritual she'd performed using a doll that resembled him. She still wasn't entirely sure what she thought about magic and witchcraft, even though she'd seen for herself what it could do.

"What are you thinking about?" Scott's voice jerked Kate out of her daydream.

"Nothing," she said quickly. "Just about how nice it is to be here with you."

"I'm sorry it's taken so long," Scott said, picking a roll from the basket in front of him and spreading butter on it. "What with school and work, and your basketball games and this whole scouting thing, I didn't think we'd ever be free on the same night."

That was something else Kate didn't want to think about—the scouting thing. Scott, a senior, was the captain of the Beecher Falls High School football team. He was a great player, and several colleges had been interested in him because of his football skills. For the past month they'd been taking him on tours of various campuses and trying to get him to agree to come to their schools. At first it had been just one school, one not too far from Beecher Falls. But then three other schools had come calling—schools that were far away—and now Scott was trying to decide which one he wanted to go to.

Kate was trying to be supportive, but she was terrified that Scott was going to end up at a school somewhere across the country. She wished she were a senior too, instead of just a sophomore. Then maybe she and Scott could go to school together. But she wasn't, and as the end of the year came closer and closer, the more she found herself wondering what was going to happen to them after graduation.

"You're worrying about the school thing, aren't you?" Scott asked, chewing on the bread.

Kate nodded, trying to not look sad. She didn't want to ruin what was supposed to be their most romantic date yet—a belated Valentine's Day dinner. They'd had to skip the real thing because Scott had gone on the first of his school visits that weekend. He'd promised to take her out later, and now they were sitting across from one another at a great restaurant and Kate was holding the beautiful red rose Scott had presented her with when he picked her up.

"I told you before," Scott said, taking her other hand in his. "It doesn't matter where I go. Whether it's here or somewhere else, we'll still be together."

"I know," Kate said. "It just seems like the year is flying by too quickly. I wish we had more time."

"We have all the time in the world," Scott said as the waitress arrived with their food and Kate was forced to let go of his hand.

They ate happily, each taking bites from the

other's plate. Then, when they were finished, the waitress appeared with two bowls of chocolate mousse covered in whipped cream and strawberries.

"Be careful," she said as she set one of the bowls in front of Kate. "The chef put some of his secret ingredients in here tonight. Make sure you don't bite down too hard."

"What does she mean by that?" Kate asked as she dipped her spoon into the chocolate.

"Got me," Scott replied. "Maybe there are nuts in here or something."

Kate took a tentative bite of the mousse, savoring the sweetness. There didn't seem to be anything unusual in it, and she took another bite. Again there was nothing. But on her third bite she felt something hard beneath her tongue, something sharp and metallic. *That's no nut*, she thought as she reached up and took whatever it was out of her mouth.

It was a ring. Kate held it in her hand, staring at it and wondering how it might have gotten into her mousse.

"Surprise!" Scott said, grinning.

Kate looked at him in confusion. "You knew about this?" she asked.

"How do you think it got in there?" Scott said, taking the ring from her and wiping it off with his napkin. "Don't you recognize it?"

He handed the ring back to Kate and she

looked at it. It was a silver ring with a small purple stone.

"It's the ring from the antiques store!" she said. A couple of weeks before, while she and Scott had been walking around town after seeing a movie, they had gone into a little antiques store to look around. Kate had seen the ring and commented on how pretty she thought it was.

"I went back and got it," Scott said. "I thought I should get you something. You know, to make up for missing the real Valentine's Day and all. Try it on."

Kate slipped the ring over her finger. "It's perfect," she said, holding her hand up so Scott could see.

"That seemed better than wearing my class ring with ten miles of yarn wrapped around it," Scott said. "Do you like it?"

"I love it," said Kate enthusiastically.

"Now you'll have something to remember me by when I'm—" Scott paused and looked down at his nearly empty dessert bowl.

The happiness inside Kate flowed out as quickly as it had come. "You *have* decided where you're going, haven't you?" she said.

Scott sighed. "Not entirely," he answered. "But New York is looking better and better."

New York. Three thousand miles away. *He might as well be going to school on the moon,* thought Kate. She looked at the beautiful ring on her finger and tried to will the sinking feeling in her stomach to go away.

"You're right," she said, trying to sound more hopeful than she felt. "It won't matter where you go. We'll still be together. And this *will* always remind me of you. I can't wait to show it to the girls."

"You and your friends," Scott said, laughing. "I'm surprised I could get you away from them for the night."

"A girl's friends are very important," said Kate. "You're a boy. You wouldn't understand."

"Probably not," Scott admitted. "But can I have another half hour or so of your time before you check in?"

"I think I can manage that," Kate said. "Maybe I'll even let you take me home."

After the last of the dessert was gone and the bill was paid, Scott stood up and helped Kate on with her coat. They left the restaurant and walked down the pier to the parking area. Scott put his arm around Kate, holding her close as they walked, and she let herself enjoy the way their bodies moved so comfortably together, as if they'd been going out for much longer than just six weeks. It was amazing how much her life had changed in that time, and not just because of Scott.

But those things were far from her mind as they reached Scott's car and got inside. They made the drive home through the downtown area and past the campus of Jasper College, around which Kate's neighborhood was based, in silence, still holding hands. Kate tried not to think about the future. Scott was right; they still had three months of school left, and then the whole summer. That was a lot of time. *Besides*, Kate thought, *a lot can happen in three months*.

Scott pulled up in front of a house and stopped. "Here we are," he said. "Door-to-door service."

"It's just like having my own chauffeur," Kate said.

"Except most chauffeurs wouldn't do this," said Scott, leaning over and kissing her.

Kate felt as if she'd stopped breathing. When his lips touched hers, she didn't want him to ever pull away. It was as if they could stop time as long as their mouths didn't part and break the spell.

But eventually Scott did pull away. "I had a great time tonight," he said. "I hope it was worth the wait."

"It was most definitely worth the wait," said Kate. "This was the best Valentine's Day date I've ever had."

"I thought you told me it was the *only* one you've ever had," Scott teased.

"It's still the best," said Kate, reaching into the backseat and pulling out a backpack. "Now I'd better get inside, or those girls are going to think we've gotten engaged."

Scott leaned over and kissed her again. "I'll call you tomorrow," he said. "Have fun tonight."

"I already have," Kate said, opening the door and getting out.

Kate walked to the front door of the house. She rang the bell, and almost immediately the door flew open and two expectant faces peered out at her.

"Well?" said Annie, pushing up her glasses in a familiar gesture. "What happened?"

"You're fifteen minutes late, young lady," added Cooper, her arms across her chest in mock annoyance.

"Sorry, moms," Kate said, pushing past her two friends and walking straight into the kitchen, where she knew there would be some hot chocolate waiting for her. Annie's rambling old house had become her second home, and Kate even had her own mug that she used whenever she came over.

"I can't believe you're not giving us the deets," Annie said plaintively, coming in right behind her.

"Deets?" said Kate, putting her backpack down and taking off her coat.

"You know, details," Annie explained.

"Since when did you get all streetwise?" Kate asked, pulling out a chair and sitting down at the kitchen table.

"She learned it from Meg," Cooper explained, sitting across from Kate.

Annie blushed. Meg was her nine-year-old sister. Where Annie was shy and reserved around other people, especially the other kids at school, Meg was a regular social butterfly, talking easily to anyone and everyone who would listen. Like Annie, she was always reading, but she'd learned to get along better in the larger world than her big sister had.

"Where is Meg, anyway?" Kate asked. Normally the little girl was at her side the minute she entered the house, anxious to tell Kate the plot of the latest book she was devouring.

"Aunt Sarah took her with her," Annie explained.

Sarah was Annie's aunt, and Annie and Meg had come to live with her after the death of their parents a number of years before. Kate still didn't know exactly what had happened to the Crandalls. Annie didn't like to talk about it, and although Kate had always wondered, she'd never felt comfortable asking. In many ways their friendship was still new, and although she, Cooper, and Annie had shared a lot, they all still had some secrets.

"Took her with her?" Kate asked, noticing a

plate of chocolate chip cookies on the table and taking one.

"To visit a friend out of town," Annie said. "They'll be back on Sunday."

"You mean we have the house to ourselves?" Kate asked, giving her friends a wicked look. "In that case, I say an all-night pajama party is in order."

"First things first," said Cooper. "We have something to show you."

Kate looked from Cooper to Annie. Sometimes she couldn't believe that the three of them were really friends. Kate was as outgoing as Annie was shy. And Cooper, with her ever-changing hair color (it had recently gone from bright pink to bright blue) and loner attitude, was the last person Kate would have ever thought she'd be spending a Friday night with. But that too, was before the whole spell thing. Now here she was, waiting for Cooper and Annie to spill the beans.

"While you were out with lover boy, Annie and I made a trip down to Crones' Circle," Cooper said, referring to the funky bookstore where the three of them had been spending a lot of time since their experience with the spell book the month before. The store specialized in books about Wicca and other esoteric topics, and they had learned a lot since first walking through the door in search of some much-needed help.

"And?" Kate said with exaggerated effect.

"And we found this," Cooper said, handing Kate a flyer printed on grass-green paper.

Kate took the flyer and looked at it, reading it out loud as she munched on a cookie. "'The Coven of the Green Wood invites you to a celebration of the Spring Equinox. Saturday, March 19. Ritual begins at five, with potluck after. Bring food to share.'"

"Doesn't it sound great?" Annie asked excitedly. "It's an open ritual. Anyone can go."

"Sophia said it would be okay if we came," Cooper added. Sophia was one of the women who owned Crones' Circle, and she had answered many of their questions about Wicca.

"I don't know," said Kate, staring at the flyer.

"What do you mean you don't know?" Cooper said irritably. "It's our first ritual."

"First one with real witches," Annie corrected.

Kate looked from one to the other. They both seemed so excited. She wished she was as sure as they seemed to be. Getting together with real witches made everything feel a lot more serious, at least to Kate, who still wasn't entirely sure what she thought about the whole subject of Wicca. She didn't know if she was ready for it.

"I'll think about it," she said, and her friends groaned. They knew that whenever Kate said she'd think about something it really meant she didn't want to do it but was afraid to hurt their feelings.

"Think fast," Cooper said. "It's tomorrow night."

"Tomorrow is tomorrow," Kate said, thinking about what Scott had said earlier in the evening. "We have lots of time. Now, don't you want to hear about this ring?"

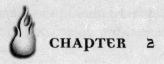

CHAPTER 2

"Not that one," Sherrie said the instant Jessica emerged from the dressing room smoothing the front of the blue flowered dress she'd gone in to try on. "You looked better in the green. Don't you guys agree?"

"Definitely," Tara responded. "The straps on that one make you look *way* too Christina Aguilera."

Kate listened to her friends' banter as they thoroughly critiqued the dress. Sherrie, ever the boss, was making Jessica turn around so that she could see how the dress looked from all angles. Jessica, who was never exactly thrilled about trying on clothes, looked like a reluctant farm animal being judged at a state fair. A farm animal with gorgeous long blond hair and sparkling green eyes.

"Come on, you guys," she said. "It's just a cello recital. It's not like I'm going to the Oscars or something. Why can't I wear plain old black like everyone else does?"

"That's the point," Sherrie said, handing Jessica

another dress and motioning her back into the changing room. "If everyone else is wearing it, you want to look different. Like Kate did at the Valentine's Day dance."

Leave it to Sherrie to bring that up, Kate thought. Sherrie, Jessica, and Tara were her oldest friends. Until recently, she would have said they were her best friends. But that was before Annie and Cooper had come into the picture. Now she wasn't always sure. Things had definitely changed after the Valentine's Day dance the month before, when Kate had shown up with Cooper and Annie, the three of them dressed like the fairy godmothers from the Disney version of *Sleeping Beauty*.

Before the dance—and before stumbling upon the spell book—Kate had spent most of her time with Sherrie and the girls. They'd been best friends since second grade, doing practically everything together. Kate was on the basketball team with Jessica and Tara, and together with Sherrie the four of them were one of the more popular groups at Beecher Falls High School. But now things were changing. Kate was spending more time with Cooper and Annie. Her old friends, particularly Sherrie, couldn't understand why she would want to hang around with girls they considered, for various reasons, two of the least suitable friends Kate could have.

For their parts, Annie and Cooper viewed Sherrie, Tara, and Jessica with a mixture of envy (on Annie's part) and disdain (on Cooper's). They could understand why Kate might want to remain part of the popular crowd, but she knew they didn't entirely get it. And she couldn't explain it to them, the same way she couldn't explain to Sherrie and the others why she liked Annie and Cooper. Both groups played important parts in her life, and she couldn't give up one for the other. When she was with Cooper and Annie, talking about Wicca, she felt they shared a secret from everyone else. But when she was with Tara, Jessica, and Sherrie, she felt a part of things, like any high school girl with a great boyfriend and a fabulous social life. She didn't have to worry about magic and what getting involved with witchcraft meant or any of that.

Kate ignored Sherrie's comment, knowing that responding to it would just cause an argument. As it was, she had managed to negotiate an uneasy truce between her two sets of friends, carefully dividing her time between them. Later today she was supposed to go back to Annie's, although she still hadn't decided whether or not she was going to the Spring Equinox ritual Cooper and Annie had tried to talk her into.

She looked at her watch. It was two-thirty. She still had some time before she had to make a decision. She'd told Cooper and Annie that she'd return around four.

"That ring Scott gave you is so pretty," Tara

cooed as they waited for Jessica to come out. "Let's see it again."

Kate held up her hand. That was another thing she liked about hanging out with her old friends—she could talk about her relationship with Scott. They'd asked her to repeat the story about the ring several times, but Annie and Cooper had listened to it once, and then with only the barest hint of interest. Cooper, in fact, refused to even call Scott by name, referring to him as "the dumb jock" or "Lover Boy." Annie was more polite, but Kate knew that she couldn't really see the appeal of Scott either.

Tara, however, couldn't stop oohing and aahing over the ring. And although Sherrie pretended to not be that impressed, Kate knew that inside she was wishing that a guy would pay as much attention to her.

"What do you guys think?" Jessica asked, stepping out from behind the curtain in the dark red dress Sherrie had insisted she try on.

Kate, Sherrie, and Jessica looked at one another. "That's the one," they said in unison.

Later, as Kate rode the bus back to her neighborhood, she thought about the Spring Equinox ritual. Did she want to go? Part of her did. But part of her was afraid. She had already taken some big steps away from the security of her old group of friends and the social world they moved in. It wasn't like she was being ostracized or anything, but she definitely felt that she didn't belong entirely to that world anymore. And, despite promising Annie and Cooper that she would give it serious thought, she really hadn't decided how involved she wanted to be with Wicca. Reading about it was fine, and doing the occasional ritual with Cooper and Annie was fun too. But she certainly didn't consider herself a witch or anything.

The bus stopped at the corner of Annie's street and Kate got off. She hurried up the sidewalk. After shopping, she and her friends had stopped for pizza, and she had lost track of time. It was already after four, and she knew that Annie and Cooper were going to be annoyed that she had kept them waiting.

But when she got to Annie's house she found a note taped to the front door.

Kate:
We've gone to the Equinox gathering. We hope you come too. We've got everything you need. Just bring yourself!
Annie and Cooper

They'd written the address on the bottom of the note. Kate considered it. The house where the gathering was taking place wasn't far away. She could easily walk there and still be on time. But she could just as easily not go and blame her absence on her lateness. In fact, if she went home she might still be able to spend the evening with Scott.

She decided to start for home, and had taken a few steps down the sidewalk when she stopped and looked at the note in her hand. She knew Cooper and Annie would be disappointed. And what was the big deal about a little ritual? *It can't be that bad*, she told herself as she switched directions and headed the other way.

The house where the Equinox ritual was being held was farther away than she'd thought, and Kate arrived at the door a few minutes before five. Part of her hoped that no one would answer the door when she knocked, giving her another excuse to go home, but a moment later the door swung open and a woman peered out at her.

"Hi," Kate said, feeling slightly foolish. "I'm here for the ritual. I'm supposed to meet my friends."

The woman smiled. "You must be Kate," she said. "Come in. We'd almost given up on you."

Kate entered the house, wondering how the woman knew her name. "I'm sorry I'm late," she said.

"Never mind," the woman said. "We're about to start. The others are in the garden. Follow me."

They walked through the house and into a large kitchen filled with delicious smells that came from the bowls and trays of food arranged on a big wooden table. *That must be for the potluck*, Kate thought. *I wonder if Annie and Cooper brought anything.*

The woman opened the door at the back of the kitchen, and Kate saw that behind the house there was a large garden area ringed by tall trees whose branches were covered in small, new leaves. An herb garden, its plants still dead from the cold of winter but with tiny, tentative, shoots poking out of the earth, took up one corner. The lawn was dotted with purple and white crocuses, and around the edges clumps of snowdrops nodded their heads on delicate stems.

A group of about twenty people was gathered in the garden. Many of them wore long white robes. Others wore robes of different colors, and a few just had on their everyday clothes. Kate scanned the faces, looking for Annie and Cooper, and found them standing together talking to a small woman with short brown hair. Kate recognized her as Archer, one of the women who worked at Crones' Circle. Annie and Cooper were wearing the robes that Kate had made for their very first ritual together. Annie's was green, while Cooper's was purple.

"Did I miss anything?" Kate asked, walking up to the three of them.

"You made it!" said Annie, sounding pleased.

"Barely," said Kate. "And I didn't bring a robe or anything."

"We brought yours," Annie said. "I left it in the house."

Kate turned to go back inside to put on her robe, but Archer stopped her. "We're about to start," she said. "But don't worry. You don't really need a robe. They're just for fun anyway."

The various conversations that had been going on stopped as a woman dressed in a simple, flowing white dress and wearing a garland of violets and daffodils on her head stepped into the center of the garden.

"We're ready to begin," she said. "If everyone will form a circle, we can get started."

The group arranged itself into a circle. As people took their positions, Kate found that she was separated from Annie and Cooper by several people she didn't know. To her right was a man with a salt-and-pepper beard, and to her left was the woman who had opened the door for her. Kate looked to see where Cooper and Annie were and saw them about a quarter of the way around the circle. Annie was sandwiched between Archer and a woman with red hair, and Cooper was several people away. A woman who could have been Kate's grandmother was on one side of her, and on the other was a boy who looked about seventeen.

Kate was surprised to see the boy there. She had expected that she and Cooper and Annie would be the only teenagers at the ritual and, apart from him, it looked as though they were. He was dressed in jeans and a blue sweater. His black hair looked deliberately messy, with one lock of it dipping over his forehead. He was thin, with pale skin and an intelligent face. Cooper, Kate observed, didn't even seem to notice him standing beside her.

The woman in the center of the circle was looking around at all of them. "Welcome to the Spring Equinox ritual," she said. "My name is Rowan, and I'm part of the Coven of the Green Wood. Some of you I've seen before, and some of you are new faces. For those of you who haven't been to one of our open rituals before, let me explain a few things. We hold open rituals four times a year—on the Winter and Summer Solstices, and on the Spring and Autumn Equinoxes. We are a coven of witches working in an eclectic style, which means we don't follow any one way of performing rituals. These are times for us to experiment with new ways of celebrating. Our rituals involve singing, chanting, dancing, and especially eating."

Everyone laughed when Rowan mentioned eating, and suddenly Kate felt a lot of the tension flow out of her. She'd been expecting the ritual to be a solemn, maybe even overwhelming, affair, and she'd been afraid that she wouldn't know what to do or say. But Rowan seemed very easygoing. Maybe it would be fun after all.

"In case you don't know what the Spring Equinox is," Rowan continued, "it's the day of the year when light and dark are in perfect balance. It also goes by the name Eostre, which most of you will probably recognize as sounding an awful lot like Easter. That's because the holiday was a celebration of the pagan fertility goddess Eostre. In those ancient days that so many pagans and witches are fond of talking about, Eostre was a time for celebrating the beginning of the planting season and a time for asking the earth goddess to bless the fields and make them abundant. Now that we buy most of our food down at Stop and Shop, we don't really need to do that. But those of us who follow the old religion still like to celebrate this day as a time of new beginnings. After the cold of winter, we all look forward to the warmth of summer, and we figure the earth can always use a little waking up after her long nap. So that's what today is about—new beginnings. Now, let's get started. Don't worry—if you don't know what to do, just watch. You'll figure it out soon enough."

Rowan took her place in the circle. She nodded to a man who had a small drum slung over his shoulder, and he began to play a steady beat on it. As he did, the people on either side of Kate took hold of her hands, and she felt them start moving to the left. She moved with them, her feet crossing over each other as the circle turned, everyone walking in time with the drumming. When the circle reached a certain point, it stopped and a woman stepped forward, holding up her hands to the sky.

"East," she said in a clear, strong voice. "Place of air. The spring breeze that whispers to the flowers and shakes them with its laughter. Welcome to our circle."

"Welcome!" came the answering cry of the others in the circle.

Kate knew that the woman was calling the directions. It was how most Wiccan rituals began, with the casting of the magic circle. The woman used words different from those Kate used when she, Annie, and Cooper did their rituals, but Kate knew that there were many different ways of casting the circle. She listened with interest as the ritual continued. They joined hands and moved a little farther around the circle. Each time they stopped, someone else stepped forward and called to a direction, just as the first woman had.

"South, place of fire," said the woman who had let Kate into the house. "Bright rays of sun that warm the earth and wake her from her sleep. Welcome to our circle."

As she always did during the calling of the directions, Kate tried to feel each one as it was invoked. She concentrated on the way the air moved around her and how the sun felt where it warmed her skin. When she did rituals inside, she often visualized herself in nature. But outside, she really felt connected to the elements. They were all around her, and as they were called, she imagined them answering, coming closer and joining the people in the circle.

"West, place of water," said the bearded man beside Kate when they stopped for the third time. "Ancient ocean and spring rain. Ever-frozen iceberg and gently rushing stream. Welcome to our circle."

At the final stop, Kate was surprised to see the young man across from her step forward. "North," he said, his voice soft and pleasant. "Place of earth. Dry desert and fertile seed bed. Tall mountain and tiny pebble. Welcome to our circle."

"Welcome," said Kate along with the others as the boy stepped back into the circle. Kate looked at him, and saw that he was looking back. Even from across the garden she could see that his eyes were a warm golden color, like the sun on autumn leaves. The boy smiled, then looked away.

Rowan stepped once more into the center of the circle. Holding up her hands, she chanted, "By the earth and by the fire, by the water and the air. Cast we now this magic circle. Joy to all who enter here. The circle is cast. We are now in sacred space. Let us—"

"Wait!" a voice cried, interrupting Rowan's next statement. Everyone turned to look, and Kate saw a girl standing in the doorway of the kitchen. About Kate's age, she was very thin, with long black hair that she tucked behind her ears as they stared at her.

"Hi," she said timidly. "Am I late?"

The girl was wearing a dark blue robe that was

too big for her. It pooled at her feet, and she kept pushing the sleeves up so that they didn't cover her hands.

I wonder why she got one so big? Kate thought to herself. Then she looked harder at the robe. *And why does it look just like mine?*

chapter 3

The girl stepped into the yard and wedged herself between two of the people closest to the kitchen door, who moved over to let her in. When the circle was re-formed, Rowan continued.

"We are now in sacred space," she repeated. "Let us begin. Would you all be seated."

Everybody sat on the ground, which, thanks to the afternoon sun, was dry. Kate had no idea what was going to happen next. She was still a little distracted, both by the fact that the boy with the golden eyes had smiled at her and by wondering why the girl who had come so late was wearing what seemed to be *her* robe. She tried to push both thoughts to the back of her mind and concentrate on what was happening.

Rowan seated herself in the center of the circle. The man with the drum sat beside her.

"I'm going to ask all of you to close your eyes," Rowan said. "We're going to do a guided meditation. Keep your eyes closed until I tell you to open them."

Kate closed her eyes and listened as Rowan began the meditation.

"Picture yourself in a small boat," Rowan began. "You're riding down a swift-moving river. You don't know where you're going, but the boat weaves its way easily among the rocks and rapids."

Rowan's voice was soothing, and Kate felt herself relaxing as she imagined herself in a little boat with a small white sail, speeding along a river in the spring sunshine. She wondered where the boat might take her, and listened for Rowan's next suggestion.

"You come to a turn in the river," Rowan continued. "All of a sudden the river opens up into a wide lake. And in the center of the lake is a small island rising up from the water, which is still and clear. The boat is still moving, and it takes you to the shore of the island. When you reach it, you climb out and walk onto the grassy bank."

Kate could feel the rocking of the boat as she stepped out of it and put her bare foot on the warm grass of the island. She was filled with a sense of adventure, not knowing where she was or what she would find there. A small breeze blew through the garden, caressing her skin, and she smelled the scent of grass and earth around her.

"Ahead of you is a path," said Rowan. "As you look at it, you hear the sound of drumming."

There was a soft thud as the man beside Rowan began to drum, his hands beating a slow and steady rhythm.

"Listen to the drum," Rowan instructed. "Follow its sound as you begin to walk the path. Let the sound of the drum guide you. The path winds around the island, taking you all along its edge. Then it begins to spiral in, making smaller and smaller circles."

Rowan continued to talk as the man drummed, and Kate let the images Rowan described come to life in her imagination. In her mind she circled the island path, the sand warm beneath her feet as she wound her way through tall grasses and swaying wildflowers, following the quiet voice of the drum as it urged her forward. She felt herself becoming more and more relaxed as the sound filled her head like a heartbeat.

When Kate had circled the island several times, the path reached the center, and Rowan told them that they were standing in the middle of a small clearing. Suddenly, the drumming stopped.

"The goddess of spring, Gaia, has come here today to welcome back her child, the sun," Rowan said. "He is growing bigger and brighter, and today he begins his journey through the sky to help make the crops grow strong. The goddess needs our help to welcome him, and she asks that we dance and sing with her to celebrate the beginning of his journey. You will hear the drum begin again. Follow its sound as you walk the path back to the shore. When you reach the entrance to the path, open your eyes. You will still be on the island, and it will be time to begin the celebration."

Kate turned and followed the spiral path back around the island, listening to the beating of the drum. When she reached the shore, she opened her eyes and looked around. She was almost surprised to find herself seated in the garden of the house, surrounded by other people. She half expected to see Gaia sitting in the center of the circle. And when she saw that there *was* someone seated there, she was startled.

Rowan was gone. In her place was a woman wearing a green robe, and on her head was a garland of flowers. She looked around at the people circled about her, smiling at each of them.

"Welcome," she said. "I am the goddess Gaia. I welcome you here now, and ask you to join me as we sing to my child, the sun."

The woman stood, and the others did likewise. She walked to a man standing near her and took his hand. "We are going to do a spiral dance," she said. "Just as you walked the spiral path of my island, now we will dance the path together. I will lead, and all you need do is follow."

The man with the drum started to play again, this time tapping out a livelier beat. The woman dressed as the goddess began to walk clockwise around the circle. As the man whose hand she held followed, he took up the hand of the person beside him. Each person in turn took the hand of her or his neighbor, forming a chain that followed the goddess as she went around the garden. As the circle turned, the woman began to sing.

"Welcome, spring, the child of sunfire. Give to us the gift of light. As you travel through the heavens, may the days grow long and bright."

The group took up the song, their voices filling the garden. Kate listened several times to the words, then joined in. The chant sounded almost like a nursery rhyme, like something children would sing on a playground. As Kate sang it, she could easily imagine the sun as a shining little boy running through the spring flowers, laughing and playing.

When the person next to her grabbed her hand, she became part of the line of people as it passed by, and found herself walking in a circle. The woman leading the dance had gone all around the garden, and when she came to the point where she had begun she moved closer to the center of the circle. Now the people at the front of the line began to pass by the people at the end, and Kate understood why it was called a spiral dance.

Kate found herself looking into the faces of those going by her as she made the first circle around the garden. At first she was a little embarrassed to have people seeing her singing, but soon she was enjoying looking at the different faces as they went by. She hadn't really had a chance to see everyone because she'd come late, but now she got to see who else had come for the ritual. There were all kinds of faces—old ones and young ones, men and women, people with long hair and some with none at all. When Annie, and then Cooper, passed by her, she gave them big smiles.

The spiral was growing tighter as the leader turned and then turned again, pulling the rings of people closer together. Kate wondered what would happen when she reached the center and couldn't go anywhere else. She tried to concentrate on the words of the chant they were singing, letting the hands on either side of her lead her.

Then she turned, spiraling in once more, and found herself looking into the face of the boy with the golden eyes. As he passed her, she heard him singing. His voice was rich and steady, and she was sorry when he moved past and she couldn't hear him anymore. Especially when she found her ears filled with a loud, off-key voice.

It was the girl in the blue robe. She was passing Kate, and she was singing very loudly and very badly. As she went by, Kate got a closer look at her robe, which kept getting tangled in her feet and was becoming covered with grass stains.

That is *my robe!* Kate thought angrily. The realization made her lose her place in the chant, and it took her a minute to pick it up again. But by that time the words had changed. They were singing something else.

"Green leaf, blue sky," sang some of the people.

"Warm sun, cool rains," sang others.

The two sets of words, both sung at once, created a beautiful blending of voices. Kate felt surrounded by a web of words that held her up as she spiraled closer and closer to the center. She watched the woman dressed as the goddess near the very middle of the garden, where she expected her to stop. Instead, as she reached the center she turned, moving counterclockwise past the person behind her and spiraling back out again.

The dance swirled one way and then another. Kate lost herself in the continually changing sea of faces and sounds. Sometimes she saw a face she recognized for a moment. She knew that she had passed Annie, Cooper, and the golden-eyed boy several times. Kate felt as if a thin ribbon of golden light flowed through the fingers of everyone in the chain, holding them together. She'd felt it once before during a ritual with Annie and Cooper, but not as strongly as she did now.

Then, almost without her realizing it, the spiral unwound and the circle was back in its original form. Everyone still held hands, and Kate looked around the circle at the faces bright with the glow of dancing.

"Move to the center and bring your hands together," the woman portraying the goddess said.

Everyone moved forward, lifting their hands into the air until they were pressed into a tight bunch.

"Release your hands and send the energy we've raised into the sky," the goddess told them.

Dozens of fingers waved in the afternoon light as the people around Kate reached for the sun.

"And now return to the circle," said the goddess.

They moved back to their original positions and sat down once more. Kate felt incredibly alive and happy. The woman playing the goddess stood in the circle, holding a big basket.

"You've helped me to welcome the sun," she said. "And now I would like to give you a gift. Long ago on this day, people dyed eggs red to symbolize the sun. The egg is a symbol of life and of creation. To help you remember what you've done here, I would like to give you each an egg. Place it on your personal altar, or wherever you can see it every day. When you look at it, remember that within each of you there is a creative force. As the season grows brighter, let that creativity within you grow into something special."

The woman walked around the circle, handing each person an egg. When Kate received hers, she was surprised at how light it was. Then she realized that probably the insides had been blown out so that the eggs wouldn't spoil. She looked at her egg. It was dyed bright red and painted with yellow and orange spirals.

When everyone had an egg, Rowan stepped into the circle once more and announced that it was time to thank the directions. Moving backward, from north to east, they said farewell to the directions and the elements they represented.

"And now let's finish with the traditional witches' farewell," Rowan concluded, and those who knew it joined her in saying, "The circle is open, but unbroken. Merry meet, and merry part, and merry meet again."

Having finished the ritual, people moved back into the house, where the food was waiting. Kate joined Cooper and Annie, and as they went into the house, the girls were joined by Sophia, their friend from the bookstore.

"So, what did you think?" she asked.

"Very cool," Cooper said.

"Yeah," said Kate. "Thanks for inviting us."

"I thought you might like it," Sophia responded. "You might also like the class that Rowan and some of the other coven members are going to be teaching at the store."

"Class?" said Annie.

Sophia nodded. "An intro to witchcraft class. It's short—only three weeks. The idea is to talk about the basic beliefs of witchcraft and what it means to be Wiccan. I know you guys have been doing some studying on your own, but this might be a good way for you to meet other people in the community."

"When is it?" asked Annie.

"Tuesday nights," Sophia answered. "From six to eight. Think you can make it?"

"I can," Annie said.

"Me too," added Cooper. "What about you, Kate? Do you have basketball practice or anything?"

"The season is just about over," Kate said. "I could go."

"Great," said Sophia. "I'll tell Rowan."

"Can anyone come?" someone asked, interrupting them. The girl in the blue robe was standing beside them. "I couldn't help but overhear," she said. "So, can anyone come to the class?"

"Well, we generally don't let anyone under sixteen join," Sophia said kindly. "But Annie, Cooper, and Kate have been doing a lot of reading on their own."

"I know a lot about Wicca," the girl said. "I've been into it since I was twelve. And I'll be sixteen in a couple months anyway."

Sophia laughed. "In that case, I guess I have to say yes, don't I?" she said. "Okay, you can come. What's your name?"

"Sasha," the girl said. "My family just moved here, and I've really been wanting to find some other pagans to hang out with."

"Well, you should start with these three," Sophia said. "They can tell you where the store is. And now I'm going to try to snag some of those lemon squares over on the table before the goddess of spring eats them all."

Sophia left the girls standing with Sasha.

"This is so cool," Sasha said. "I had no idea there were so many witches in Beecher Falls. Are you guys a coven, or what?"

"Not exactly," Cooper said. "So, you just moved here?"

"Yeah," said Sasha. "My dad's in software development. We just moved here from LA."

"Will you be going to Beecher Falls High?" asked Annie.

"I guess," Sasha said. "I mean, yeah. That sounds like the school my mom mentioned."

"If you don't mind my asking," said Kate. "Where'd you get the robe?"

"This?" said Sasha. "I found it on a chair in the kitchen when I came in. I didn't think anyone would mind. Do you like it?"

"I should," Kate answered. "I made it."

Sasha turned red and began to take off the robe. "I'm really sorry," she said. "I didn't mean to—"

"It's okay," Kate relented. "You can keep it. It looks good on you."

Sasha grinned. "Thanks," she said. "Man, I'm so happy to meet you guys. I didn't think I'd meet any cool people here. Hey—do you guys want something to eat? I'm starved."

The four of them headed for the food table. As Kate perused the bowls of potato salad and the various steaming vegetable and tuna casseroles, she watched Sasha. She was piling food onto her plate as fast as she could. *She eats a lot for such a skinny thing,* Kate thought. She didn't know why she'd told Sasha that she could keep the robe. It had just come out. Something about Sasha made Kate want to be nice to her.

Kate was reaching for the spoon to take some pasta salad when someone else reached for it and bumped her hand.

"Sorry," she said.

"You first," said a guy's voice.

Kate looked over and saw the boy with the golden eyes standing beside her.

"Hi," he said. "I'm Tyler."

"I'm Kate," she said. Then she couldn't think of anything else to say, so she just stood there, feeling stupid.

"Are you guys going to hog that salad all night?" someone said, pushing between them. It was Sasha.

Kate looked across Sasha at Tyler and shrugged her shoulders. Before she could say anything else a young woman came up and tapped him on the shoulder.

"We've got to go," she said. "The concert starts in half an hour."

Tyler put down his plate, waved at Kate, and followed the woman to the door. As he walked away, Kate found herself with all kinds of questions. Who exactly was Tyler? Why was he at the ritual? Was the woman his girlfriend? Why did she care anyway? She had a great boyfriend. She was even wearing the ring he gave her.

Still, as she spooned pasta salad onto her plate, she couldn't stop thinking about the boy with the golden eyes.

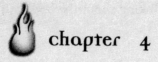 chapter 4

On Monday morning Kate walked into Beecher Falls High School feeling better than she could ever remember feeling on the first day of a new week. She didn't have any tests, she'd finished her math homework and her essay for English, and best of all, her boyfriend was waiting for her at her locker.

"Hi there," he said, giving her a kiss. "I've missed you."

"It's only been twelve hours," Kate teased.

After spending Saturday night at Annie's again, she'd gone home the next day for her usual routine of church and Sunday dinner with her family. Then it had been time for homework, followed by an early movie with Scott. All in all, it had been a fantastic weekend.

"Well, I missed you anyway," he said as Kate put her coat away and grabbed the books for her morning classes.

Scott took her hand and began walking Kate to the chemistry lab where she had her first period class. As they rounded the corner, Kate nearly ran over Sasha, who was coming the other way.

"Hey there!" Sasha said brightly. "Just the person I was looking for."

Scott looked at Sasha, who was dressed in old jeans, a faded flannel shirt, and a jacket that was too big for her. "Who's your new friend?" he asked. Kate could tell by his tone that he wasn't sure what to make of the girl standing in front of them.

"Oh, um, this is Sasha," Kate explained. "She just moved here with her family."

"Dad's in software development," Sasha said to Scott, then she turned her attention to Kate again. "So, you going to show the new girl around on her first day?"

"Sure," Kate said, trying to sound friendly. The truth was, she'd forgotten all about Sasha's starting classes at Beecher. Besides, the school office usually assigned someone to show new students around, and she really didn't want to be saddled with Sasha for the day. But she also knew that it must be hard being the new girl in school, and she didn't want Sasha to feel all alone.

"I'll leave you two to get to it, then," Scott said. He leaned over and gave Kate a quick kiss. "See you later."

As Scott walked away down the hall, Sasha watched him go. "What a hottie," she said to Kate. "Have you two been going out long?"

"About six weeks," Kate said.

Sasha nodded knowingly. "Still in the honey-moon period," she said. "I give it another month before he's driving you crazy."

"Do you have a boyfriend?" Kate asked.

"Oh, yeah," Sasha replied. "Back in LA. He's great—a drummer in this ska band. They're really good. They even opened for No Doubt once. This is his jacket I'm wearing. See, it has his name on it."

Kate looked at the jacket. "Jack" was stitched in red thread over one pocket, and there was a grease stain beneath it.

"He works in a garage when he's not playing," Sasha explained, seeing Kate looking at the stain.

"You must miss him," said Kate, thinking of Scott and where he might be in six months.

Sasha shrugged. "If you really love someone, it doesn't matter where he is, right?"

Kate thought about it for a moment. "I guess not," she said. "But I'd rather not have to find out. What's your first class?"

"I think they told me I'm in the same class you're in," Sasha said.

"Chemistry," Kate said.

"Sounds like a drag to me," replied Sasha.

"It's okay," Kate said. "And Annie's in it too. She's a lot more into it than I am, though."

"Then I guess she's the one to ask for homework advice," said Sasha. "You're the boyfriend expert and she's the brain. Got it."

Kate laughed in spite of herself. Sasha had a

good sense of humor, and although she was a little rough around the edges, Kate liked her spirit. *Maybe she'll turn out to be okay*, Kate thought as they went into the chemistry class.

It turned out that Sasha and Kate had several classes together. Sasha appeared in Kate's fourth period English class as well, where she ended up sitting in the seat behind Kate. They were studying American writers, and when Mrs. Milder asked Sasha to name her favorite, she said it was a toss-up between Stephen King and John Grisham. Her answer brought a laugh from the class, but the teacher didn't seem impressed and suggested that Sasha look over the reading list and pick something a little more literary to do her semester paper on.

"I can't believe she doesn't think Stephen King is great literature," Sasha said as she and Kate walked to the cafeteria for lunch after class. "Hasn't she ever read *The Shining*?"

"I think *The Scarlet Letter* is more her thing," Kate suggested as she looked to see who else was in the cafeteria. She spotted Jessica, Tara, and Sherrie at their usual table, and waved.

"Are those your friends?" Sasha asked.

Kate nodded. "One set of them," she said. "It's a little complicated."

"Let's sit with them," Sasha suggested. "They look cool."

Kate hesitated. She knew Sasha wasn't exactly the kind of girl Sherrie considered worthy of hanging out with. Kate already got enough grief from her for being friends with Annie and Cooper. Adding Sasha to the list might be the last straw. But she also had a feeling that Sasha could hold her own when she needed to, and she'd learned a lot about standing up to Sherrie in the past month, so she walked over to the table and sat down.

"Hey, guys," she said. "This is Sasha. She's new in school, and I'm showing her around."

Almost immediately, Sherrie started in. "You're new?" she said, as if she couldn't believe that someone was walking around school without her knowing it.

"We just moved here," Sasha explained.

"From LA," added Kate, knowing that Sherrie would think a newcomer from Los Angeles was something to get excited about.

"Where are you living now?" Sherrie continued, pretending not to be impressed.

"We haven't found a place yet," Sasha answered. "My mother is really fussy about houses. We're staying with some friends until she finds exactly the right thing."

"Aren't you eating?" Jessica asked Sasha, noticing that the other girl didn't have a lunch with her.

"Nah," Sasha explained. "I'm on a diet. I want to lose five pounds before swimsuit season."

"Oh, you should try one of these, then," Jessica said, pointing to the pile of potato chips she'd spread out on her napkin. "Totally fat-free. I'm sure they're made out of chemicals that would pickle lab rats, but who cares? They taste great."

"Thanks," said Sasha, taking a handful of chips and eating them eagerly.

Sherrie took a bite of the fruit salad on her tray. "Who wants to hear the latest gossip?" she asked coyly.

"Like you have to ask?" Tara retorted.

"Sherrie is the complete source for all the news at Beecher Falls High School," Kate explained to Sasha. "She knows what's happening before it even happens."

"This time I just might," Sherrie said smugly. "Word is that Mark Davis is going to dump Kathy Lewis."

"No way!" said Tara, the cupcake in her hand frozen on its way to her mouth.

"But why?" asked Kate, interested despite herself. "They've been going out since forever."

"Apparently, Mark found a love note that Kathy wrote to someone else," Sherrie said.

"Who?" asked Jessica, wide-eyed.

"That part I don't know," Sherrie admitted. "Yet. But give me a couple of hours."

"Wow," said Sasha. "You really do know it all. I could have used you last night. I was trying to get the story on this guy I met. A real cutie. But he was with this girl, and I couldn't figure out whether they were together or what. You saw him, Kate. That guy with the far-out eyes."

"Kate saw him?" Sherrie said.

"Yeah," Sasha answered. "We were both at this rit—"

"At this party," Kate said, suddenly interrupting. "Sasha and I were at the same party. That's how we met."

"You didn't tell us about a party," Tara said accusingly.

"It was probably something her *other* friends were involved in," said Sherrie.

"You mean Annie and Cooper?" Sasha said. "Oh, yeah, they were there too. It was great."

"I'm sure it was," said Sherrie, staring hard at Kate.

"It was no big deal," Kate said hurriedly. "Just this little thing that Annie's aunt threw together."

"Whatever," said Sherrie. "So, Sasha, tell us about this guy."

Sasha started describing Tyler to the other girls, starting with his black hair and moving on to his clothes and even his shoes. As she talked, Kate tried to think. It hadn't occurred to her that Sasha might say anything about the ritual. So far Kate had managed to keep all of her Wiccan activities away from the prying eyes of her friends. She would have to make sure that Sasha knew the topic was off-limits before she said something that got Kate into trouble.

Part of Kate was also jealous that Sasha had noticed Tyler too. She'd been careful not to mention him, even to Annie and Cooper. They were always giving her a hard time about Scott, and she didn't want them to think she was totally boy crazy. Besides, it wasn't like she wanted to go out with the guy or anything. She just thought he was cute. Clearly, so did Sasha.

"Oh, and he had the best smile," she was saying when Kate returned to the conversation.

"Sounds dreamy," Tara said. "Unlike the trolls who go to this school."

"I don't know," Sasha said. "I think Kate's man is pretty studly."

"Yes, our little Kate managed to land quite a fine one," Jessica said. "We're very proud of her."

"We still don't know quite how she did it," Sherrie said, never content to let anyone else get the attention.

"Maybe she cast a spell on him," Sasha suggested, helping herself to more of Jessica's potato chips.

"Didn't you want me to show you the library?" Kate said to Sasha, trying to create a diversion. She didn't want Sasha to mention spells or rituals or witchcraft in any form before she could talk to her.

Sasha looked confused. "I don't think—" she began. Then she saw the intense look on Kate's face. "Oh, right. Do you want to do that now?"

"I think it would be a good idea," Kate said, getting up. "We have a few minutes before the next class."

Sasha stood to follow Kate. "It was nice meeting

you guys," she said. "I guess I'll see you around."

The others said good-bye, and Kate and Sasha walked out of the cafeteria. As soon as they were in the hallway, Kate started talking.

"It might be better if you didn't mention anything to Sherrie, Tara, and Jessica about the party we went to last night," she said.

"You mean the ritual?" said Sasha.

Kate looked around, making sure that no one had heard her. "Yes," she said. "That. They don't know anything about that kind of thing. Most important, they don't know that *I* know anything about it."

"Got it," said Sasha. "You're still in the broom closet."

"What?" said Kate.

"The broom closet," Sasha repeated. "You haven't told anyone that you're a—you know—witch." She whispered the last word, then laughed.

"But I'm not," said Kate.

Sasha stopped and looked at her in surprise. "You mean you just happen to go to Wiccan rituals and hang out with witches?" she said.

Kate sighed. "It's a long story," she said.

"I have time," Sasha responded.

"Not here," said Kate. "Come on."

She led Sasha down the hall and opened the door that led to the school basement. The practice rooms for the music students were down there, and Kate knew that it would be quiet. She found an empty room and drew Sasha inside, shutting the door behind them.

"Here's the deal," she said. "About six weeks ago I found this book of spells in the library. I didn't know what it was. Just for fun, I tried one. It worked a little too well, and I needed some help stopping it. That's where Annie and Cooper came in. They had checked the book out, too, so I asked them to work with me to reverse my spell. We managed to do it, but it was really rough for a while. After it was all over, we agreed to keep studying witchcraft."

"I get it," said Sasha. "And you were at the ritual because you read about it somewhere."

"Right," said Kate. "Annie and Cooper got a flyer at Crones' Circle."

"Now it makes sense," said Sasha. "I thought the three of you were some kind of coven or something."

"Hardly," Kate said. "The spells we've done haven't exactly been great successes. Scott's the only good thing that came from any of it."

"So you *did* cast a spell on him!" Sasha crowed in delight.

"At first I did," Kate admitted. "But he stuck around even when it was over, so there had to have been more to it than that. At least I hope there was."

"Who cares?" said Sasha. "The point is, you got what you wanted, right? That's what this stuff is all about."

Kate wasn't sure she agreed with Sasha, but she

didn't say anything. It wasn't the time to get into a philosophical discussion about magic.

"We don't talk about Wicca at school," she said, trying to get to the main point of the conversation. "I don't think people here really get it, and we don't want to get into any trouble."

"That's cool," Sasha said. "No witch talk in front of the other kiddies. But you've got to do me a favor in return."

"What's that?" Kate asked.

"Tell me about that boyfriend spell," Sasha said. "It sounds like a doozy."

Kate laughed. "Later," she said. "Right now we have to get to class. Do you know where you're going?"

"Yeah, I've got it down now," Sasha said, hoisting her bag over her shoulder. As she did, Kate realized that Sasha had been carrying the same bag around all day. She also still had on her coat.

"Don't you want to put any of that in your locker?" she asked. "It looks heavy, and you must be really hot in that coat."

"It's okay," Sasha said. "I like keeping it all with me. You never know what you might need."

They left the practice room and walked back upstairs, parting at a corner in the corridor as Kate headed for her history class.

"Let me know if you want to walk home after school," Kate said. "Which direction do you go?"

"Don't worry about it," Sasha said. "I'm meeting my mom for some shopping. I'll catch you later."

"Okay," Kate said, turning and walking to class. She was glad that Sasha was turning out to be pretty nice after all. *It just goes to show*, she thought to herself, *you can't always judge people on first impressions.*

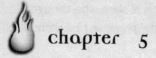

chapter 5

The back room at Crones' Circle was filled with people on Tuesday night. Some were sitting on the old purple velvet sofa. Some were seated in folding chairs. Still others were sitting cross-legged on cushions that Archer was dragging out of a storage room.

"I didn't know there would be so many people here," Annie said to Kate as they walked in.

"Hey, guys," Archer said, noticing them standing in the doorway. "Grab some cushions and join the fun."

"Thanks," Kate said as Archer gave her a hug. She was particularly fond of the wiry, talkative woman with the quick wit. Archer had given Kate some good advice, along with a surprisingly accurate Tarot card reading, when Kate was trying to figure out what to do about her friendship with Annie and Cooper.

"Are you teaching the class?" Cooper asked, taking a cushion and finding an open spot on the floor.

"No," said Archer. "Rowan, from the Coven of the Green Wood, is doing this one. We just provide the space."

Archer went to greet some other people, and Kate, Cooper, Annie, and Sasha sat down. Almost immediately, a fat gray cat padded over and jumped into Cooper's lap.

"Simeon," Cooper said, scratching the cat behind the ears as it started to purr and knead her with its paws. "Nice to see you."

"This place is great," Sasha said, looking around. "It's even got its own cat."

Kate looked around the room to see who else had come for the first class. She was a little worried that she might see someone who knew her or knew her family, and she'd already worked out a story to tell anyone who might wonder what she was doing there. She was going to say that she was doing research for a school project. She'd told her parents that she was going to a study group for chem class. Having to make up stories bothered her, but she knew she couldn't tell them where she was really going.

But she didn't recognize any of the dozen or so people crowded into the small room. Most of them seemed to be students from Jasper College, judging by the sweatshirts they wore and the backpacks they carried with the college logo on them. There was one woman who had to be at least seventy, and there were a couple of men sitting together on the couch. Kate breathed a sigh of relief that no one looked familiar to her.

A woman came into the room and walked to the front. It took Kate a moment to realize that it was Rowan. She was dressed in jeans and a black turtle-neck, and without the white robe and garland of flowers Kate almost didn't recognize her.

"Good evening," she said, and the various con-versations in the room stopped. "Welcome to the first class in our Exploring Witchcraft series. My name is Rowan, and I'll be one of the people lead-ing the discussions. Some of you I've seen before, and some of you are new faces. I hope that by the end of the class I'll know all of you a little better. Now, just to get an idea of where people are, can I get a show of hands from people who have any experience practicing witchcraft."

About half the class raised their hands, includ-ing Annie, Cooper, and Sasha. Kate hesitated for a moment, then raised hers as well. Outside of rituals and talking to Archer, Sophia, and the other women at the bookstore, she'd never publicly associated herself with Wicca. She felt a little thrill of excite-ment as she saw that the people who weren't rais-ing their hands were looking at her and the others curiously.

"Good," said Rowan. "That gives me a better idea of where to begin. Now, before we start, I want to explain how the course works. We'll have three classes. On the fourth Tuesday, we'll be performing a dedication ritual. Those of you who would like to dedicate yourselves to studying Wicca more seriously can participate."

"You mean we'd become witches?" Sasha asked.

"No," Rowan explained. "It takes a little more than three or four weeks of studying before you know enough to decide whether or not you want to devote yourself to a life in witchcraft. This is simply a dedication ceremony. You would agree to spend a year and a day living a Wiccan life and studying the Craft in greater detail. We'll actually be holding weekly meetings for those who are interested. At the end of that year and a day, you could decide to become witches if you wanted to."

"What if we don't want to take part in the ceremony?" asked a woman sitting to Kate's left. "Should we not take the class?"

"Oh, no," said Rowan. "Anyone can take the class. If you don't want to be part of the dedication ritual, that's fine. It's just an option for those who want to."

The woman nodded. Rowan waited to see if anyone else had questions. When no one spoke, she continued.

"Tonight we're going to talk about what witchcraft is and isn't," she said. "Why don't we start with the word *witch* itself. Does anyone know what it means?"

"Doesn't it mean a wise person?" asked one of the men on the couch.

Rowan nodded. "That's one of the meanings. There are several origins for the word. One is from the Old English word *wicca* or *wicce*, which referred to men or women who practiced divination and had other skills thought to be somehow supernatural. These skills might have been as simple as knowing how to use herbs to heal people, which in those times might indeed have seemed supernatural. There's also the word *witta*, which meant a sage or an adviser. The word *witch* probably has its beginnings in those words."

"What about warlocks?" someone asked Rowan. "Isn't that what male witches are called?"

Rowan smiled. "A lot of people think that," she said. "But male witches are witches, just like female ones are. The word *warlock* actually means 'traitor' or 'one who breaks an oath.' The term was applied derogatorily to men accused of witchcraft because people said that they had turned away from God. But real witches never use that term."

There was something Kate had been confused about ever since doing her school paper on witchcraft. She raised her hand and waited for Rowan to acknowledge her. "I know witchcraft is really old," she said. "But did witches way back when really do things the way people do them today? Did they worship a goddess and all of that?"

"You've just asked the million-dollar question," Rowan said. "This is the thing that many, many people get hung up on—what exactly is witchcraft, and where did it come from? That's a long story, but I'll try to give you the short version. Many people will try to tell you that the witchcraft practiced today has been handed down from generation to generation, and that the rituals and chants and invocations we use today are ancient secrets practiced by our ancestors."

"You mean they aren't?" Cooper said.

Rowan shrugged. "Who's to say?" she answered. "Probably some of them have some basis in ancient rituals. But the truth is that what we call witchcraft today is a mixture of all kinds of things. Some of it comes from ancient fertility rites. Some of it is based on old legends and myths. And some of it we've just made up in the last fifty years."

"Doesn't that mean that witchcraft isn't real?" said the old woman seated in one of the armchairs. "I mean, if it's all made up, what holds it together?"

"Witchcraft is a religion," Rowan said. "But it isn't a religion centered around one particular book, like the Torah or the Koran, or around one particular figure, like Jesus or the Buddha. That's what confuses a lot of people. Witchcraft is a pagan religion, meaning that it doesn't focus on only one god or goddess. It's a religion based on rituals and festivals practiced by people who lived in close communion with nature. But it is also a changing religion. People bring to it the various rituals and beliefs of their respective cultures. Unlike Christianity and Judaism, which have established sets of rules and basic beliefs, witchcraft has very few set beliefs. Different witches practice it differently. Some do magic. Others don't. Some worship particular gods and goddesses. Others don't worship any at all."

"Then what holds it together?" asked Annie.

"A basic belief that everything in the world is connected somehow to everything else, and that becoming more attuned to these connections, and to the cycles of nature, can bring great changes to your life," Rowan answered. "I know that sounds like a non-answer, but it's true. Witches believe that, because everything is connected, what we do with our lives creates changes all around us. We believe that by becoming more aware of the natural processes of life and nature we can learn to work with those processes to effect change. We might use magic to make these changes. We might use chanting and singing and drumming. We might use meditation. But whatever we do, what we're trying to accomplish is the same—we're trying to make positive changes in our lives and in the world we live in."

"That makes witchcraft sound really boring," Sasha said. "What about all the robes and candles and incense and all of that? Where's the fun stuff?"

"You can't look at just the trappings and costumes of ritual," Rowan said. "Those things are fun, but the real power of witchcraft is in the changes that take place when you dedicate yourself to understanding the rhythms and cycles of nature—and to exploring your connections with the world and how those things can have an effect on your own life and on the lives of others."

"I still like the robes and the incense," Sasha whispered to Kate. "This other stuff sounds too eggheady for me."

Kate was thinking about everything that Rowan had said. It was all complicated.

"How do you know if you're doing it right?" she asked, speaking her thoughts out loud.

"Another good question," said Rowan. "Again, that's going to be different for different people. And it's going to take time for you to know when something is working and when it's not. But basically you know you're doing it right if it's making your life better. If you're a happier person because of your involvement with witchcraft, and if you're living a more well-rounded and full life, then you're doing it right."

"Or if you land a great boyfriend," Sasha said to Kate, giggling.

"I don't think that's exactly what she meant," Kate responded. But she had to admit that having Scott as her boyfriend *did* make her feel better about herself. So maybe that was part of it after all.

Rowan continued. "I know you all have a lot of questions," she said. "What witchcraft is and isn't can't be explained all at once, and it will become more clear to you the more you study and learn. I've copied some reading materials for all of you which will explain a little bit more about the evolution of modern witchcraft. You can take these home and read them during the week. But for the rest of tonight I want to break into smaller groups for discussion. I'll lead one of the groups. Other members of the Coven of the Green Wood will lead groups as well. You can ask them about their own experiences in the Craft, and that might give you a better idea what this is all about. So let's form four groups of three or so people. Try to get into groups with folks you don't know. That way you'll get to know more people."

People stood up and began to form little groups. Annie and Cooper moved away from Kate and found others to stick with. Kate looked around. Almost everyone else had already matched up with a group. She noticed that the older woman was still alone, so she walked over to her and introduced herself.

"I'm Lea," the woman said. "It's nice to meet you."

"Why don't we form a group around the chair here?" said a voice behind Kate.

She turned and saw Tyler standing there, looking at her.

"I'm your leader tonight," he explained when Kate looked puzzled. "I may be young, but I've been raised in the Craft all my life. Rowan is my mother."

That explains why he was at the ritual, Kate thought. But who was the girl he had left with? She still didn't have an answer to that question. Not that it was any of her concern.

"Mind if I join you?" Sasha asked. "All the other groups are full."

"Not at all," Tyler said. "Let's sit down."

They all sat around Lea's chair and started talking. Tyler explained to them that his mother had been a member of the Coven of the Green Wood since before he was born. He had been brought up participating in rituals, and had joined the coven himself when he was thirteen.

"Did you ever think about becoming something else?" Kate asked.

Tyler nodded. "I learned about a lot of different religions while I was growing up," he said. "I went to Jewish synagogues and Muslim mosques. I went to Baptist churches and Catholic churches and Quaker meetings. My sister and I learned Buddhist meditation and different things like that. But I always came back to witchcraft. It just feels right for me."

"You have a sister?" Sasha asked.

"Yes," said Tyler. "She's over there with one of the other groups."

Kate looked in the direction Tyler was nodding. When she saw that his sister was the girl from the ritual, something inside of her breathed a sigh of relief. *She wasn't a girlfriend after all. Why am I even thinking about that?* Kate thought, scolding herself. She ran her finger absentmindedly over the ring that Scott had given her. When she looked up, she saw that Tyler had turned his tawny eyes in her direction. She looked away, pretending to scratch her nose.

They talked for a long time about Tyler's experiences as a witch. Lea was very interested in knowing how he felt about being part of such a misunderstood religion. Sasha asked some questions about magic. But Kate kept quiet. She didn't really know what to ask. Plus, she was afraid that if she said anything Tyler would look at her again, and she didn't know if she could take it.

When Rowan announced that time was up, the groups broke up and people went to pick up the handouts that were sitting on the table at the front of the room. Kate was standing with Sasha, waiting for her turn, when Tyler walked up to them.

"Kate," he said. "You're awfully quiet. I was wondering if you had any questions of your own. Maybe you'd like to get together during the week to talk more about things. Or maybe I could call you."

Kate looked at him. She wasn't sure, but she thought he was asking her out. For a moment she felt the peculiar tickling sensation in her stomach that she'd had the first time Scott had asked her out. But then she came to her senses.

"I don't know," she said. "I'm going to be really busy this week."

Tyler nodded. "That's okay," he said. "We can talk next week."

"I have some questions," Sasha said suddenly. "Maybe you and I could get together. I'm not too busy this week."

Kate looked at Sasha in surprise. She was clearly trying to get Tyler to ask her out. But he deflected her. "Maybe we should save all the questions for class," he said. "I'll see you guys next week."

After he left, Sasha turned to Kate. "I can't believe he just asked you out," she said. "And I can't believe you said no."

"But I have a boyfriend," Kate said. "And so do you. What about Jack?"

"Who?" Sasha said absentmindedly as she stared at Tyler's retreating back. "Oh, Jack. You're right. But I wasn't really asking Tyler out. I was just trying to help him save face after you rejected him."

"Thanks, I guess," said Kate.

"No problem," Sasha replied. "But I still can't believe you said no. You've got all the luck—two gorgeous guys who have it bad for you. The least you could do is share one with the rest of us."

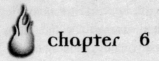 chapter 6

On Wednesday, Kate arrived at Annie's house earlier than she'd expected to. Coach Saliers had been in one of her rare good moods and had only made them do light drills and play a short scrimmage before sending them to the showers. Kate had declined an offer from Jessica and Tara to go watch a video afterward, telling them that she had some homework to do. But the truth was that she wanted to talk to Annie in private.

She rang the bell and waited for someone to answer, hoping that Annie would be home alone. But when the door opened and she saw Sasha's face peering out, she was shocked.

"Hey," Sasha said. "Come on in."

Kate entered the house and followed Sasha into the kitchen, where Annie was just taking something out of the oven. Annie was always trying out new recipes, mixing ingredients together as easily as she combined chemicals in lab experiments. As usual, the room was filled with smells that made Kate's mouth water.

"Hi," Annie said. "You're just in time. Sasha and I made peanut butter cookies."

"They're my favorite," Sasha explained. "I showed Annie how to make the little crosshatch design on the top with a fork. Want one?"

"No, thanks," Kate answered, putting her backpack down. "I'm not hungry." She really would have liked to have had some cookies, but she was annoyed that Sasha was there. She needed to talk to Annie alone, and now she wouldn't get to. Besides, since when had Annie gotten to be so friendly with the new girl? After-school get-togethers had always been reserved for Cooper, Annie, and Kate. Now Sasha was acting as if she'd always been part of the group, and even though she liked Sasha, that bothered Kate a little.

"Sasha and I were talking about last night's class," Annie said. "I thought it was really interesting."

"Yeah," said Sasha, taking a still-warm cookie and popping it in her mouth. "We're going to do the dedication ritual. Are you?"

Kate didn't know what to say. She honestly hadn't thought about it much at all. But apparently Sasha and Annie had, and they'd been talking about it.

"I think Cooper wants to do it too," Annie said.

"She does," Sasha said. "I talked to her about it in school today."

"I didn't see you in class today," Kate said. "I

thought you might be sick or something."

"I just missed the morning classes," Sasha explained. "I had to do some stuff with my mom. But Coop and I have math together seventh period. That's when I saw her."

Coop? thought Kate. Nobody called Cooper "Coop."

"I haven't really decided if I'm doing it or not," Kate said. "The ritual, I mean. It sounds like a big step."

"Come on," Sasha urged. "We're all doing it. You can't be the only one left out. Besides, then maybe you can spend more time with Mr. Golden Eyes."

"Who?" Annie asked, sliding cookies off a cookie sheet and onto the counter.

"You know," Sasha said. "That guy who has the hots for Kate. I told you about him."

Annie nodded. Kate felt anger rise up inside her. "I really don't like people talking about me when I'm not around," she said, more harshly than she'd intended.

Sasha raised her hands. "Sorry," she said. "I didn't mean to tell tales out of school. I thought it was just between friends."

"That's okay," Kate said, feeling bad for blowing up. "I didn't mean to snap at you. I just had a long day. Maybe I do need one of those cookies after all."

Sasha pushed a plate of cookies toward her, and Kate took one. After finishing it, she felt a little better. After finishing three, she felt great. She sat down at the table across from Sasha.

"Maybe it's just the cookies talking, but I think I *will* do the dedication ritual," she said. "It might be fun." Some of her uneasy feelings had died away, and she was feeling more comfortable. Maybe the ritual really would be fun. Besides, if her friends were all doing it, she didn't want to feel left out.

"That's the spirit," Sasha said. "Then the whole gang will be officially witchy. Everyone at school will be in awe of our powers."

"I didn't say anything about telling people at school," Kate said.

"Right," said Annie. "We had enough trouble when one little spell went wrong. No one even knew we were responsible, but they blamed us anyway. If they actually knew we were involved in Wicca, they'd just assume everything was our fault."

"You guys worry too much," Sasha said. "Back in LA, no one cared if you were a witch or not. I had lots of witch friends in school. We called ourselves the Coven of Angels. You know, because Los Angeles is the City of Angels."

"I don't think something like that would go over very well in Beecher Falls," Annie said seriously.

"I know it wouldn't," Kate added. "Besides, no one in my family knows, and I'd like to keep it that way."

"It's your call," Sasha said. "I just think it would

be cool to be able to walk around school with everyone knowing that we're witches."

They sat at the table talking until the last sheet of cookies was cooling on the counter. Then Sasha asked if she could see Annie's bedroom.

They went up the narrow staircase that led to Annie's attic bedroom. When Sasha saw it, she gave a long whistle.

"This place is cool," she said. "You have this whole thing to yourself?"

Annie nodded. "All mine."

Sasha walked around the room picking things up and looking at them. She ran her hands over the quilt on Annie's bed and stood looking out the big windows that offered a view of the treetops and, far beyond them, the ocean. Then she put her arms out and spun around a few times in the center of the room.

"I can't wait to do rituals in here," she said. "Imagine, your very own secret space. I'd give anything for a room like this."

She stopped twirling and went over to one of Annie's bookshelves. Looking at the books, she picked one out and held it up.

"Is this the spell book that started it all?"

"That's the one," Kate said. "The good old 'Come to Me Love Spell.'"

Sasha flipped through the pages, looking for the spell. When she found it, she read for a few minutes, then laughed. "This sounds like a bunch of bad poetry," she said. "It really worked?"

Annie and Kate both nodded. "Kate had every guy in school after her for a while," Annie said.

"I didn't even know what I was doing," said Kate. "I just thought it might be fun."

"But look at you now," Sasha replied. "You must have done something right."

"I don't think Scott's going out with me has anything to do with the spell," Kate said. "I think it just got him interested."

"But don't tell Cooper that," Annie said, teasing her friend. "She still says Scott has to be the most willing subject of a spell ever."

A buzzing sound from downstairs interrupted their conversation. Sasha jumped up. "That must be the timer," she said. "I left it on so we'd know how long the cookies had been cooling. I'll go turn it off."

"That's okay," said Annie, getting up. "I'll go. You stay and talk to Kate."

Annie left, and Sasha threw herself on the bed, stretching out. "I'm so glad I met you guys," she said. "I really miss my friends back home, but you make it a lot easier."

Kate wasn't sure what to say. Was she glad that Sasha had come into their lives? She wasn't sure. She liked her, but there were times when the other girl got on her nerves a little. But was it because she was annoying, or just because she was different? Kate couldn't tell yet.

"Hey, what time is it?" Sasha asked suddenly.

Kate looked at her watch. "Almost five-thirty," she said.

"I've got to go," Sasha said, sitting up. "I told the woman at the shelter that I'd be there by six."

"Shelter?" Kate asked, confused.

"Yeah," Sasha answered. "I do this volunteer thing. You know the Summer House?"

Kate nodded. The Summer House was a home for runaways, many of whom came to Beecher Falls on their way to Seattle. Kate's mother sometimes donated food from her catering business to them.

"I go there sometimes," Sasha explained, picking up her backpack. "I volunteered at a shelter in LA, and I really liked it, so when I came here they hooked me up with the Summer House. But the lady running it hates it when we're late, so I have to scoot."

Sasha ran out of the bedroom and took the stairs two at a time. She said good-bye to Annie and headed for the front door. Kate heard it slam shut before she herself had even made it to the kitchen.

"She was sure in a hurry," Annie said. "I was just bringing up more cookies."

Kate explained where Sasha was going. "I can't quite figure her out," she said when she had finished the story.

"What do you mean?" asked Annie.

"Well, she's just kind of weird," Kate said.

"A lot of people think *we're* weird," Annie reminded her. "And as I recall, you thought Cooper and I were really weird before you met us."

"You two *are* weird," Kate said. "I'm the only normal one in this crowd."

"What brought you over here, anyway?" Annie asked. "I thought you'd be out with the Graces or something." "The Graces" is what Annie had taken to calling Sherrie, Jessica, and Tara, after the three Graces of Greek mythology. Given the girls' interest in being beautiful and popular, it was an appropriate title, and it had quickly become Annie and Cooper's shorthand for them.

"I wanted to talk to you," Kate said. "But not in front of Sasha."

"Sounds serious," said Annie. "Do I need to be sitting down?"

Kate rolled her eyes. "No. It's just boy problems. Not even boy problems really. Just something I don't know what to think about."

"Did something happen with Scott?" Annie queried.

Kate shook her head. "No. He's fine. Great. It's this other guy."

"The one Sasha was telling me about?" Annie asked.

"That's the one," Kate said. "The boy with the golden eyes, as I keep referring to him in my head. Tyler."

"What about him?" asked Annie.

"That's just it," said Kate. "I don't know. He asked me out, sort of, and I said no. And I really meant it.

71

But then I find myself thinking about him a lot."

"Thinking in an I-wish-he'd-kiss-me kind of way?" Annie asked. "Or just an I-think-he's-sort-of-cute kind of way?"

Kate rested her chin in her hands. "I thought it was the second kind," she said. "But when he asked me out, a little tiny part of me almost said yes before the bigger part stopped me." She took a cookie from the plate and bit into it. "What does it mean?" she asked.

"Don't look at me," Annie said. "No one has ever asked me out."

"Come on," Kate wailed. "You're the brain around here. You must have *some* rational way of figuring this out."

Annie thought for a moment. "Maybe there is a scientific way to approach this," she said. "Let's make lists."

"Lists?" said Kate. "What kind of lists?"

"Pros and cons," said Annie. "For Scott and Tyler."

She went into another room and returned with a pad and pen. She wrote Scott's name at the top and Tyler's name halfway down the page. Then she drew a line down the center and wrote "pros" on one side and "cons" on the other.

"Now, start thinking," she said to Kate. "What are the pros of being with Scott?"

"He's cute," Kate said instantly, and Annie wrote it down under Scott's name.

"What else?" she asked.

"He treats me really well," Kate said, thinking. "He has a car. He looks great in a football uniform."

"I think that's covered under cute," Annie said.

Kate thought of a few more things. Then Annie told her to think of the cons of dating him.

"He's probably leaving at the end of the summer," Kate said. "That's all I can think of."

"I wish Cooper were here," Annie said. "She'd come up with a laundry list. But let's move on to Tyler. Pros."

"His eyes," Kate said instantly, then paused.

"He's Wiccan," Annie suggested.

"I guess that's a plus," Kate said. "Put it down."

She thought of a few more things to write down about Tyler, and then they moved on to the cons.

"He's not Scott," she said immediately.

"That doesn't count," Annie said. "It's like a double negative or something. Think of something else."

Kate thought, and added a few things to Tyler's con list. When she was done, Annie showed her the lists.

"Seems to me that all Tyler has over Scott is that he'll be here come September and he has great eyes," Annie said. "Is that enough?"

Kate shook her head. "No," she said. "It isn't. So why do I keep thinking about him?"

"I can't help you there," Annie said. "But science

doesn't lie. Statistically speaking, Scott is ahead by about fifty points."

"You're right," Kate said. "I have a great boyfriend."

"You don't sound entirely convinced," Annie said. "Do you want me to go over the lists again?"

Kate shook her head. "I think I'm just scared," she said.

"Of Scott's leaving?" Annie asked.

"More of Scott's changing, I guess," Kate answered. "He's going to be in college and living somewhere new. He's going to be doing all kinds of exciting things. What if he decides he wants something else—or someone else?"

"Now I get it," Annie said. "You're afraid he won't be satisfied with a girlfriend back home who's still in high school when he's going to parties with college girls who would love to go out with the hot new football player."

"That makes me feel *so* much better," Kate said. "Thank you for putting my deepest fears into words."

"Sorry," said Annie. "But look at it this way. You were afraid he would never go out with you in the first place, and you were wrong about that. Clearly the boy sees something in you that he likes. Why should that change?"

"Maybe it won't," Kate admitted. "Maybe I'm just being ridiculous. I guess maybe I saw Tyler as a fall-back plan in case things with Scott didn't work out. But you're right. I shouldn't worry about it. And who knows—maybe he won't leave after all." She glanced at the clock. "I'd better get going too. It's almost time for dinner."

"Aunt Sarah and Meg should be home from the library soon too," Annie said. "Meg will probably have fifteen new books she'll want to read to me. I'd better get all of these dishes washed up."

"Thanks for listening to me be stupid," Kate said.

"Any time," Annie replied. "Now, go call that boyfriend of yours. He might think you've run off with someone else if you don't talk to him every hour or so."

chapter 7

The wind coming off of the ocean made Kate shiver, and she pulled the ends of her sweatshirt's sleeves over her hands. Sitting on the rock, watching the waves roll in, she thought about the night when she, Cooper, and Annie had done their ritual in the little cove. It had been the ritual that ended the confusion caused by her spells. They had each given up something to the ritual fire that night, and Kate could still see the smoke rising up toward the full moon.

There was no full moon tonight. The weather had turned stormy on Thursday, and it was still gray and windy on Friday evening. Kate had been surprised when Scott suggested that they go to the beach. She thought he would want to see a movie or maybe go out with some of the other football players and their girlfriends. But there they were, sitting side by side on a huge boulder that stretched out into the ocean and was reached by climbing up a series of smaller, steplike rocks. It was Kate's favorite spot on the beach. Sitting up there made her feel like she was stranded on a deserted island. But she wasn't alone. Scott was with her. It was just the two of them and miles of ocean and sky. She reached for his hand, and relaxed as his fingers closed around hers.

Ever since her conversation with Annie, Kate had been happier with Scott than ever. Sasha had been right—she was lucky. Scott was a great guy. And she'd decided that she wasn't going to worry about the future until it happened. She had no way of knowing what might happen a week, a month, or a year from now. All she could do was enjoy the time she and Scott still had. The future would take care of itself.

"It's so beautiful out here," she said, leaning her head against Scott.

Scott didn't say anything in response. When Kate looked at him, he was staring out into the distance.

"Are you okay?" she asked. He'd been quiet ever since he'd picked her up.

"Yeah," he said. "Just thinking about stuff."

"That's never a good sign," Kate teased, but Scott didn't laugh.

"Kate, I've made a decision," he said.

Kate looked at the waves. Something in Scott's voice made her nervous. "About what?" she asked, afraid that she already knew the answer.

"About school," he said. "I've decided to go to New York."

Kate felt her hands grow damp, and she hoped Scott wouldn't notice. She waited a minute, composing herself. Trying to sound as normal as possible, she said, "It's a good school."

Scott nodded. "I know," he said. "It has a great program, and the coach has taken the team to the championship three years in a row. I really think it's where I need to be."

Kate knew that Scott was right. All along she'd suspected that he would pick New York. But until he'd said it, she hadn't realized how much she wanted it to not be New York. Now that the choice was made, she wanted to try to be as grown-up about it as she could be.

"There are always holidays," she said, hoping her voice sounded enthusiastic. "Besides, I've always wanted to go to a Broadway show. Now I'll have two reasons to fly out there."

Scott let go of her hand and put both his hands in his pockets. "I knew you'd understand," he said.

Kate put her arm around him. "And we still have the whole summer," she said. "We'll just have to make enough memories to last you until the first break."

Scott looked at her and gave a weak smile. "That's another thing," he said. "I don't think there will be a first break."

"What do you mean?" Kate asked, confused. "Do you have to play right through Christmas?"

Scott sighed. "Man, this is harder than I thought it would be," he said.

"What is?" Kate asked. "I already said it was okay."

"That's just it," Scott said. "It's not okay." He ran his hands through his hair.

"I just don't think this can go anywhere," he said. "You can't come to New York, and I don't think seeing each other only on holidays is enough."

"I knew it," Kate said to herself, forgetting that she was talking out loud. "I knew this would happen. I knew it was too good to be true."

Ever since she, Cooper, and Annie had done the final ritual, she'd been waiting for things with Scott to fall apart. She wanted to believe that his liking her had nothing to do with the magic. But another part of her had been waiting for the spell to wear off. Now, apparently, it had. She figured it was her punishment for having played around with something she had no business fooling with.

"What do you want me to say?" Scott asked. "I'm sorry."

"Me too," said Kate, rubbing her hands together as a chill crept over her. She felt the ring Scott had given her on her finger and took it off.

"Take this back," she said. "I don't want it."

"Keep it," Scott said. "I want you to have it."

"But I don't want it," Kate said, suddenly angry.

"I don't want anything that reminds me of you."

She threw the ring at Scott as hard as she could. It hit him in the chest and bounced off. There was a soft click as it struck the rock, and then the ring sailed off into the air. It hung there for a second and then dropped without a sound into the ocean below.

Tears filled Kate's eyes as she stood up and ran down the rock steps to the beach. Scott got up and ran after her, but she didn't stop. Her feet slipped in the sand as she ran toward the wooden stairs that led up to the parking area.

"Kate!" Scott called after her, but the wind drowned out the sound of his voice, and the sobs that came from her throat surrounded her like storm clouds.

She reached the steps and ran up them as quickly as she could. When she reached the parking lot she kept running past Scott's car and toward the bus stop. Luckily, there was a bus pulling in as she ran up. It stopped and opened its doors, and Kate ran on, barely able to find her bus pass in her coat pocket.

She stumbled to a seat and fell into it, burying her face in her hands. She didn't care who was around her or who saw her crying. She'd never felt so miserable in her entire life. As the bus pulled away from the stop, she caught a glimpse of Scott running beside it, trying to flag it down. For a moment she was afraid that the driver might stop, but he didn't, and she got away safely.

She didn't want to go home. She knew her mother would want to know why she was upset, and she didn't think she could pull herself together in time to fool her. She couldn't go to Sherrie's or Jessica's or Tara's. They were the last people she wanted to discuss her romantic woes with. As it was, Sherrie would most likely know within the hour anyway. She probably had hidden cameras on the beach.

Kate found herself getting off at the stop near Annie's house. Lately it seemed she was always going to Annie with her problems. But she felt safe in Annie's house. Annie's aunt made Kate feel like part of the family, but she never asked embarrassing questions or pried into the girls' lives. Kate just hoped that Sasha wasn't there. But recently she had spent every afternoon volunteering at the Summer House, so probably she wouldn't have time.

Kate was relieved when Annie opened the door. She took one look at Kate and pulled her inside.

"You look awful," she said. "What happened? Shouldn't you be with Scott?"

Kate started crying all over again, unable to tell Annie what was wrong. She just stood there, tears running down her face, until Annie put her arms around her and hugged her. That made her cry even more, but she felt better anyway.

"I think we . . . broke . . . up . . .," Kate said haltingly as she sobbed in between words.

"Broke up?" Annie said. "Why?"

Kate sniffled, composing herself. "I don't know," she said. "I mean, not really. He's going to school in New York."

Annie handed her a tissue to wipe her eyes with. Then she led Kate into the living room, where Meg was sitting on the couch, reading.

"Are you okay?" Meg asked Kate. "You look sad."

"I am," Kate said, trying to smile at the worried little girl.

Annie's aunt walked in a moment later. "I thought I heard you, Kate," she said. "Is everything all right?"

"Boy trouble," Annie explained, and her aunt nodded.

"I'll leave you two alone, then," she said. "If anyone wants me, I'll be in my study doing . . . something."

Kate laughed despite how she felt. Annie's aunt always knew when to disappear gracefully.

"You don't have to go," she said. "I'm okay."

"I'll go anyway," Sarah said. "If I stay too long I'll start crying, too, and no one needs that."

She left the girls alone with Meg, who went back to her book, occasionally casting glances at Kate and frowning.

"I can't believe you guys broke up," Annie said. "Everything seemed to be going so well."

"That's the thing," Kate said. "Just last night we

were making plans for the weekend. I had no clue this was coming. It's like he just froze me out while we were sitting there."

"Maybe he's just freaked out about the whole school thing," Annie said.

"But I told him I didn't mind waiting," Kate said. "And he said he didn't mind, either. At least that's what he said last week."

"There's got to be some other reason for it," Annie said. "I know boys are flaky, but they don't usually just drop girls they've recently given rings to for no reason, do they?"

"I didn't think so," said Kate. "But something's gotten into him."

"Maybe a bad witch cast a spell on him," said Meg.

Kate looked over at the little girl. "What?" she asked.

"A bad witch," Meg repeated. "Like in the fairy stories. See."

She held up the book she was reading. It was a collection of fairy tales. Meg was looking at a picture of a prince. He was in a castle dungeon, and an old, ugly hag was pointing a finger at him.

"The witch made the prince think she was a beautiful princess," Meg explained. "She made him fall in love with her. But then he woke up and saw that she was just a bad witch."

Kate looked at Annie. All along she'd been afraid that it was her spell that was keeping Scott around. Was this another sign that she'd been right?

"Upstairs," Annie said quickly. "Meg, Kate and I need to do something in my room. You stay here, okay?"

Meg sighed. "Okay," she said. "But remember what I said about the bad witch."

The two girls ran up the stairs to Annie's room, shutting the door behind them.

"Do you think Meg is right?" Kate asked. "I mean, I was thinking the same thing on the bus. Maybe Scott really is just waking up from the spell I put on him. Maybe he never liked me at all."

"I guess it's possible," Annie said. "Weirder things have happened. But it seems strange that it took this long to come to an end."

"It's true," Kate said dejectedly. "I *am* a bad witch. I'm just like one of those witches in the fairy tales. I enchanted Scott and got him for a while, but now the spell is over and he sees me the way I really am—old and ugly." She started to cry again.

"Well, that's a little dramatic," Annie said. "You're hardly old. Or ugly. But the basic principle might still apply."

"Thanks a lot," Kate said. "You're supposed to be making me feel better, not worse."

"Sorry," said Annie. "I'm trying. I'm not good at this, you know."

"Where's the spell book?" Kate asked. "The one I used in the first place. I want to read that spell again. Maybe it will give me a clue to what happened."

Annie walked to her bookshelf and started looking for the book. She ran her finger down the spines,
stopping where the book was kept. When she turned
around, she had a puzzled look on her face.

"That's weird," she said. "It's gone."

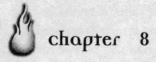 chapter 8

The weekend was terrible. Kate and Annie had been unable to find the spell book anywhere. On Saturday, Kate had tried to avoid leaving the house as much as possible, but in the afternoon she made the mistake of answering the phone, thinking it might be Scott calling to talk things over. But it had been Sherrie. Somehow she'd found out about the breakup.

"Of course, I wanted to hear it directly from you," she said. "You know how these stories can get totally twisted around."

Especially when you tell them, Kate thought. But she knew that it was better for Sherrie to have the real story. If she didn't, she'd just make up something that was a lot worse than the truth. So she told her friend what had happened.

"I told you not to trust a senior boy," Sherrie said, and Kate could just imagine her sitting in her room as she said it, shaking her head sadly. "But don't worry—we'll find you a new one in no time.

I know at least a dozen boys who would be happy to go out with you. Scott will be so jealous he'll beg you to come back."

"I don't want him to beg me to come back," Kate said.

But when she hung up, she wondered if maybe she did want Scott to want her back. Maybe she did want him to tell her that they'd made a terrible mistake and that he couldn't imagine living without her. Would that make her feel better about everything? She wasn't sure, but something about the idea appealed to her.

Something else still bothered her about the breakup. She was trying hard to convince herself that it was Scott who was making the mistake. But maybe it wasn't Scott. Maybe she had made a mistake in the first place by using magic to get him to notice her. Maybe the breakup just meant the magic had finally run out. It was possible that Scott had never really been interested in her in the first place. She'd been letting herself believe that the spell was over and that Scott was with her because he wanted to be. But now she thought she might have been wrong all along, and that the breakup was what she deserved. That was even harder to take than the idea that they'd split up because he was going off to college.

She was able to distract herself on Sunday by helping her father at his sporting goods store after church. Putting price tags on cans of tennis balls normally bored her out of her mind, but on that particular day the repetition of picking up a can, running the pricing gun over it, and putting the can on the shelf lulled her into a state of half consciousness in which she was able to not think about anything at all.

But then Monday had come. Just as she'd feared, the news about her breakup with Scott was already all over school. When she walked to her locker, she found Tara, Jessica, and Sherrie waiting for her with mournful expressions on their faces.

"I am *so* sorry," Jessica said, putting her arm around Kate.

"Sherrie told us what happened," Tara added. "And if you ask me, Scott's a big loser."

"I've already made up a list of potential new boyfriends," Sherrie said. "Do you want to go over them?"

"Later," Kate said. "But thanks for the thought."

The rest of the day was a blur, mainly because Kate spent every moment trying not to run into Scott. Besides, she got tired of everyone acting as if someone had died. Cooper was the only person who didn't offer her condolences. "Good riddance," was her succinct appraisal of the situation, and for once Kate appreciated her friend's cynicism.

The only other person who didn't seem upset for Kate was Sasha. "It's sad and all," she said at lunch. "But he's just a guy, right?"

Kate wished she could be as independent as

Sasha seemed to be. When she liked a guy, she wasn't afraid to say so. But she didn't seem to need them around her, like Sherrie did, or to hide her interest in them, the way Cooper did. She just took them as a matter of fact.

As for Scott, he'd kept a low profile all day. Kate had only seen him once, as she was walking to history after lunch, and he had turned and gone the other way when he noticed her coming.

"Running away with his tail between his legs," Sasha said, then made sounds like a dog scurrying off in fear, making Kate smile in spite of her unhappiness.

By Tuesday night, Kate was feeling better. If Scott wanted this breakup, that was fine with her. It didn't matter if the reason had been the spell's wearing off or something else. The fact was, she didn't need him around to be happy. For once she was going to take a lesson from her friends. If Sasha could be independent, then so could she. As she walked into Crones' Circle for the second witchcraft class, she was determined to have a good time.

There were fewer people at the second class. Kate noticed, as she and her friends took their seats, that some faces were missing. She quickly made note that Tyler was there again before looking away unconcerned. She was glad to see Lea was still there, though. Something about the way the older woman carried herself appealed to Kate. *I bet she's never waited around for any man*, Kate thought, giving Lea a smile.

The second class was led by Anya, another member of the Coven of the Green Wood. Anya was a thin, almost bony, woman with brown hair that she wore in two long braids. She moved her tiny hands like bird wings when she talked, and watching her made Kate think of a sparrow hopping from tree to tree.

"Our topic tonight is magic," Anya said. "Last week we talked a little bit about what witchcraft is. When most people think of witchcraft, they think of magic. So we thought we'd spend a little time talking about what magic is, what it does, and what it should and should not be used for."

Anya picked up a pot that had a small plant growing in it. "This is a lavender plant," she said. "I grew it from seeds that I started indoors about a month ago. When it's warm enough, I'm going to plant it in my garden."

Kate didn't understand what Anya was getting at. Sure, a lavender plant would be pretty, but it was hardly magic.

"It took a lot for that little seed to become this plant," Anya continued. "The seed contained everything it needed to make the plant, but without the help of the water and the light, it would have stayed dormant. And without more of it, the plant won't bloom and fill my garden with its fragrance. In a way, magic is like the water and the light. We have the potential to make all kinds of things happen. But if we don't find ways to use that potential—to nourish it—then nothing happens."

"You mean the magic is already in us?" asked a woman in the back.

"That's right," Anya said. "Many people mistakenly think of magic as something mysterious or supernatural. It is, in a way, because it's something extraordinary. But true magic is simply finding ways to make the things happen.that we already have the ability to make happen."

"Can you give us a concrete example?" asked Lea.

Anya thought for a moment. "Suppose I need money," she said. "Maybe I need six hundred dollars to pay for repairs on my car. I might do a spell in which I ask for money to come my way. A few days later, I might get a raise at work, or someone who owes me money might pay me back. I might even get a tax refund I didn't know was coming."

"But that's not magic," the first woman said. "That's just luck."

"Is it?" asked Anya. "What is magic? It's removing the obstacles that are preventing you from getting what you want or need. When I do a ritual or cast a spell, I'm really asking for help in finding ways around the obstacles that are in my way. If I need money, I look for ways that I can get that money. I don't expect it to just fall out of the sky."

"But what if you just want something?" Sasha asked. "I mean, like what if you see a really great leather jacket, but you can't afford it. Shouldn't you be able to do magic and just get it?"

"That's a good question," Anya said. "Do you think you should?"

"Sure," said Sasha. "If I can do magic, I should be able to get what I want out of it."

"What do the rest of you think?" Anya asked.

Kate thought about the question. She certainly had experience getting something she wanted with magic. And she could definitely confirm that sometimes what you ended up with wasn't at all what you thought it was going to be. But she didn't really want to tell the whole class her story, so she kept quiet. She looked at Annie and Cooper, and she knew they were thinking the same thing. After all, they all been through the experience with the mixed-up spells together, and they'd all done magic that had backfired in one way or another.

"I don't think you should use magic like a credit card," Annie said carefully, breaking the silence. "If all you do is take, take, take, then what's the point?"

"The point is that you have what you want!" Sasha said. "Why should you have to work so hard for everything when there's magic?"

"These are all good arguments," said Anya. "And they all bear discussion. What we're going to do tonight is break into groups again for a special exercise. If you can, stay with the group you were in last time. If someone from your group is gone, then just go with another group."

Kate tensed. She'd been dreading seeing Tyler again, and now she was going to have to be in a group with him. So far she'd managed to avoid talking to him since coming into the class. But now she found herself seated in a group with him. He was holding an envelope in his hands.

"This is our assignment," he explained, waving the envelope at the others. "In here is a piece of paper with a problem on it. We have to come up with a magical way of solving the problem."

"Great, a magical SAT test," Kate griped.

"Kate, why don't you open the envelope and see what our problem is?" Tyler suggested.

I already know what my problem is, Kate thought. *Guys.* She took the envelope from Tyler and opened it.

"'You're having problems with someone at work or school,'" she read. "'For some reason, the person seems to have it in for you and is making your life miserable. What kind of magical work can you do to make things better?'"

"I know what I'd do," Sasha said instantly. "I'd come up with something to make the person really sorry for being mean to me. Maybe a spell to make her unpopular."

"That might not be the best way to go," Lea suggested. "Remember, witches believe that whatever kind of energy you send out comes back to *you* three times as strong. If you send out negative energy, you might find yourself on the receiving end."

"Then, what would *you* do?" Sasha asked. "If the

person is determined to get you, I don't see what other choice you have."

"Maybe the other person is unhappy," Lea suggested, "and is just taking out all of that frustration on you."

"Or maybe she's mad at you because she thinks you did something you didn't really do," suggested Kate, thinking about her own experiences with magic gone astray.

"How would you address those things with magic?" Tyler asked.

Kate thought for a minute. "I might do a ritual where I imagined all of my own anger at the person flowing out of me and being replaced by good thoughts about her," she suggested.

"Or maybe you could work some kind of a spell designed to make her feel better about herself," Lea said. "I've certainly had a lot of trouble in my own life with people who treat others badly because they're unhappy about something."

"That seems like a waste of time," Sasha said. "I like the more direct approach. You see something you want—you get it. You need something fixed—you fix it."

Anya was walking around the room, listening to the different groups talk. She was standing by Kate's group when Sasha spoke.

"Kate and Lea are right," Anya said. "Sometimes the answer to a problem has to be found in an unexpected place. You might think the answer is to somehow stop the person who's giving you a hard time. But it might work better to try to establish a different kind of relationship with her instead. Remember what we talked about—magic should be used for removing obstacles, not for plowing through things like a bulldozer."

"I still think my way is better," Sasha said. "I've done lots of spells, and they've always worked out just fine."

"Really?" said Tyler. "What kind of spells?"

Sasha shrugged her shoulders. "All kinds," she said. "Spells to get money. Spells to get things. Spells to make people stop talking about me. Once I did this spell where I took a picture of a girl who had taken something from me and I set it on fire. The next night, her house burned."

Everyone looked at Sasha in shock.

"Oh, it was okay," Sasha said. "She didn't die or anything. It just burned down her house. But she deserved it, right? I mean, she stole stuff from me."

"I think it's time to hear how the other groups made out," Anya said. "Why don't we all go back to our seats."

The groups broke up, and Anya continued the class. She asked different people how their exercises had gone. Most of the groups had found interesting solutions to their problems. Kate found it intriguing to see how different people approached their challenges. She'd never really thought about all of the different ways that magic could be used.

Like Sasha, she had sort of seen magic as a way to make things happen more easily. But looking at it that way had gotten her into a lot of trouble, and she knew that it wasn't the way to do things.

As shocking as Sasha's revelations had been, maybe she did have a point about something. Maybe there were times when it was important to just go for something you wanted. Maybe, instead of waiting around for Scott to ask her out in the first place, she should have just asked *him*. She'd been too afraid to do that. She was afraid he would say no, or that he would laugh at her. She was afraid that people would make fun of her if they found out that she had asked a guy out.

But why shouldn't she ask a guy out? Why should she wait around for him to ask?

She glanced over and noticed Tyler sitting a few people away from her. He was watching Anya intently, nodding as she spoke. Kate looked at his face. He really *was* cute. And he had asked her out.

She tried to concentrate on what Anya was saying. But her mind kept going back to Tyler. Would it hurt her to go out with him? But she'd just broken up with Scott. It hadn't even been a week! She was supposed to be all brokenhearted. But why? Why should she sit around crying just because a guy was too stupid to know a good thing when he saw it?

Anya was ending the class, but Kate hadn't heard anything she'd said during the past five minutes. As soon as people started getting up, Kate walked over to Tyler, who was helping to put away the folding chairs. Her heart was beating a mile a minute. *So, this is what it feels like,* she thought as she tried to think of what to say. *I wonder if this is how guys feel when they ask us out.*

"Hi, Tyler," she said.

He turned and looked at her. Suddenly she felt frozen to the spot. She almost said good night and walked away, but then she thought about getting what she wanted and not being afraid.

"I know I said I was busy last week when you asked if I wanted to get together," she said, trying to keep her voice steady. "But this week is a lot better. So I was wondering if you still wanted to do that. Get together, I mean."

Tyler smiled. "Sure," he said. "How about Thursday?"

"Thursday?" said Kate, trying to think.

"You know, the night before Friday. I have something on Friday, but Thursday is good for me."

"Thursday is great," Kate said. "How about we meet here at six?"

"Six it is," Tyler responded. "See you then."

Kate turned around and saw Annie, Cooper, and Sasha watching her with big grins on their faces.

"You go, girl!" Sasha whispered.

"I knew you could do better than Dumbo," Cooper added.

"And you did it all without magic," Annie said proudly.

"I did, didn't I?" Kate said, realizing exactly what she'd just done. "I think that calls for a little celebration. Let's go to the ice cream place around the corner. Double scoops on me."

chapter 9

Kate had been reading the same paragraph for fifteen minutes. She was standing in front of one of the shelves at Crones' Circle, passing the time by looking at a book about moon rituals. But she couldn't concentrate, and finally she closed the book and put it back. She wandered over to a mirror and checked her hair in it.

"You look fine," said Tyler, coming up behind her unexpectedly.

Kate blushed. "I didn't hear you come in," she said.

"Apparently," said Tyler. "Are you ready to go?"

"Sure," said Kate. "What did you have in mind?"

"I don't know," he replied. "You asked me out, remember? I figured you'd have the whole thing planned out. But you didn't even bring me flowers."

Kate laughed. "Fair enough," she said. "Well, how about we grab something to eat at the burger place by the pier?"

Tyler agreed, and they walked down the street

toward the waterfront. At six, it was already getting dark, and the twilight sky was purple and gray. Inside the restaurant, Kate led Tyler to a booth in the back and sat down.

"I love this place," she said. "My father used to bring me here when I was little. They make great shakes."

"I'll have to try one," Tyler said. "My mom is a strict vegetarian, so we don't usually eat in places like this."

"Your mom seems really great," Kate said as the waiter brought them menus and glasses of water.

"She is," Tyler said. "She's actually fun to hang around with. I know that sounds weird, but it's true."

"It's not weird," Kate said. "I like my parents too. Only I could never talk about you-know-what with them."

"You-know-what?" Tyler asked.

"Witchcraft," Kate said in a low voice.

Tyler laughed. "Oh, that."

"My parents would never get it," Kate said. "You're lucky that your parents do."

"Only my mother," Tyler said. "My father is actually very anti-Wiccan. In fact, he tried to take my sister and me away from my mom when they divorced."

"He did?" Kate said, surprised. "Can they do that?"

Tyler nodded. "It happens a lot. He tried to

convince the judge that my mother was practicing some kind of weird religion or that she was in a cult. My sister and I had to go to psychologists and psychiatrists and take all kinds of tests showing we were normal and healthy and happy before the court would let her keep us."

"Do you still see him?" Kate asked.

"Oh, yes," Tyler said. "Every other weekend. That's what I'm doing tomorrow night, in fact. He's taking us to the opera."

"Sounds dull," Kate said.

"It's actually okay once you get used to it," Tyler said. "The worst part is when he goes on and on about how wacky pagan people are. He thinks all of my mom's friends are crazy. And the worst part is, he makes my sister and me go to private school."

"That explains why you're not at Beecher Falls," Kate said. "I was wondering about that."

"Part of the divorce agreement was that my sister and I have to attend St. Basil's," Tyler said.

"A Catholic school!" Kate exclaimed.

"My father thinks it will save us from my mother's influence," Tyler said. "But my mother thinks it's kind of funny. The nuns are all terrified of her because she comes in wearing her pentacle and insisting that Rebecca and I be excused on pagan holidays."

The waiter came to take their order, so Kate had a minute to take in what Tyler had said as he ordered a cheeseburger with mushrooms and jalapeño peppers. She tried picturing him dressed in his Catholic school uniform, but the image just wasn't right. All she could picture was how he had looked calling the directions at the Spring Equinox ritual.

"And what can I get for you?" the waiter asked, snapping her out of her daydream.

"Oh—um—a hamburger with bacon, lettuce, and tomato, please," Kate said. "And a mint chocolate milk shake."

"Make that two shakes," Tyler said. "I hear I shouldn't miss that."

"Coming right up," the waiter responded, taking their menus and leaving.

"My parents would totally freak out if they knew about me and Wicca," Kate said. "They nearly had kittens when I had my ears pierced without telling them. If I became a witch, it would be the end."

"Most people just don't understand it," Tyler said. "They think we all run around dressed in black hats and putting curses on people."

There was a pause as the waiter returned with their orders. Kate took a bite of her hamburger and watched as Tyler tried his. He chewed a mouthful and then gave her a thumbs-up.

"Excellent," he said. "Sometimes I forget what real meat tastes like. Mom is into textured vegetable protein and tofu hot dogs. They're good, but it's just not the same. So, are you going to become a witch?"

Kate choked on her mouthful of food. Tyler's

question was unexpected. She swallowed, clearing her throat, and took a long drink of her shake.

"I don't know yet," she said. "It's a big step."

"How did you get interested in Wicca anyway?" Tyler asked.

Kate paused. She didn't know what she should tell him. She didn't want to get into the whole story about Scott, the spell, and everything that had happened afterward. That would mean explaining what had happened more recently between her and Scott, and she definitely didn't want to bring *that* up.

"I checked out a book on witchcraft from the school library," Kate said. "I thought it was interesting, and I noticed that Annie and Cooper had also checked it out. I went to talk to them, and we just kind of became friends."

Okay, she thought, so it was the edited version of the story. It was basically the truth. Tyler didn't really need to know all of the grisly details. Especially not the part about her screwing up the spell and having to fix things.

"Your friends seem really great," he said. "What about Sasha, though? You don't seem to be as close to her."

"She's sort of new to our group," Kate explained. "Her family just moved here. I guess she heard about the ritual and showed up. I don't know much about her. Why, does she seem strange to you?"

"Not strange, exactly," Tyler said. "She's what some people call a 'Buffy witch.'"

"What's that?" asked Kate. "I've never heard anyone say that."

Tyler laughed. "It's sort of a joke," he said. "It means someone who has watched too many episodes of *Buffy the Vampire Slayer* and thinks witches are all about making supernatural things happen. They like to dress up in weird costumes and hold elaborate rituals, but they don't really understand what witchcraft is."

"So you don't think she can actually do magic?" Kate asked.

"I didn't say that," Tyler said. "A lot of people can do magic who maybe shouldn't be doing it. You don't have to understand something to use it."

Kate had to agree with him about that. She hadn't had any idea what magic could do when she'd tried her first spell. But she'd learned her lesson quickly, and she was trying her best to figure out what it was all about before she did any more.

"What was your first spell?" Kate asked.

Tyler snorted. "I tried to turn my sister into a frog," he said.

"Get out," Kate said. "You did not."

"I swear," Tyler said. "I was about four years old. I had no idea what I was doing. I just made up all of this mumbo jumbo and told her she was going to turn into a frog by midnight. A couple of hours later she started hopping around the house, sticking her tongue out and asking for flies. I really thought I had done it, and I was scared to death. I begged my mother to turn her back again. But of course she was just teasing me."

"Okay, what was the first *real* spell you did?" Kate asked.

"I did a spell to get my parents back together," Tyler said, sounding serious.

"And?" asked Kate.

"And it didn't work," he said. "At least, not the way I wanted it to. They ended up deciding that we would all take a vacation together at this cabin in the woods to celebrate my birthday, even though my parents had barely spoken since their divorce. Of course, they ended up getting into a huge fight, and everything was even worse than it had been. I was really angry and didn't understand why it had happened that way. I thought I must have done something wrong. But I couldn't tell my mother what I'd done. I knew she'd be mad. So I told one of the other women in the coven. She explained to me that I'd tried to do magic to get something that *I* wanted, not something that was necessarily supposed to happen. So I kind of got what I asked for— my parents got together, but only for that weekend. And it was a disaster. I learned a big lesson from that."

Kate had finished her burger and was picking at her fries thinking about how comfortable she felt listening to Tyler talk about his life and about his experiences with Wicca. She could never talk that way with Scott, who wouldn't understand the first thing about her interest in witchcraft. At first she had been afraid that no guy would want to go out with her if she was open about what she was doing. But now she was sitting with someone who not only understood it but had more experience with it than she did herself.

What would it be like to have a Wiccan boyfriend? She tried to imagine going to rituals with someone who understood what they were about, or talking with someone about spells she wanted to try. Would it be too weird? Or would it be like any two people who were dating and who shared common interests?

"Do you want to go for a walk?" Tyler asked her, interrupting her thoughts.

"Sure," Kate said. "How about the beach?"

She hadn't been to the beach since her breakup with Scott the week before. For some reason that now seemed like a lifetime ago, although she didn't know why. Was she really already over him? Or was she just trying to convince herself of that? She really didn't know for sure.

She and Tyler walked down the steep wooden stairs to the beach, then walked along the edge where the water rushed up onto the sand. As the waves came in, they waited until the last minute and jumped out of the way, laughing.

"Wait until Beltane," Tyler told Kate. "The coven holds this big ritual where everyone ends up jumping into the waves at the end. Then there's a big bonfire on the beach and we drum and chant all night. Some people even jump over the fire. It's really amazing."

"Right out on the beach?" Kate said, surprised. "Doesn't anyone complain?"

"One of the coven members has a house on the ocean," Tyler explained. "It's a private beach, so we don't have to worry about that."

"It sounds like fun," Kate said.

"Then you'll have to come," Tyler said.

"It's a date," Kate replied.

A big wave came in and Tyler jumped back, pulling Kate with him. She stumbled into his arms, and the next thing she knew his face was only inches away from hers. Even in the darkness she could see the light reflected in his eyes.

He's going to kiss me, she thought breathlessly, and opened her mouth. But as Tyler leaned toward her, she saw the outline of the giant boulder where she and Scott had broken up. She remembered the first time he had kissed her, and she pulled away from Tyler.

"I'm sorry," she said. "I just can't."

"Did I do something wrong?" Tyler asked, sounding bewildered.

"No," Kate said. "No, you didn't. I just can't, that's all."

She looked at Tyler standing in the moonlight. She wanted to rewind her life to thirty seconds before, when she was looking into his face and knowing he was about to kiss her. But she couldn't. Part of her was still with Scott, and that part of her wouldn't let her kiss Tyler.

"I should go," she said. "I know this sounds weird; I really did have a great time. But I just can't do this right now."

Before Tyler could say anything, she started walking toward the steps and the bus that would take her home.

chapter 10

The library was almost empty when Kate arrived on Saturday morning. A few students wearing Jasper College jackets were sitting at a table with notebooks spread out in front of them, but otherwise the place was deserted.

They're probably all still sleeping in, Kate thought as she looked for Sasha. She herself would probably still be in bed, too, if Sasha hadn't asked her if they could meet as early as possible so that Kate could help her with an assignment for English class. They were supposed to be doing a report on an American writer, and Sasha was having trouble getting her material organized. Kate had suggested that they meet at the house where Sasha was staying, but Sasha had suggested the library instead.

"But why did it have to be at nine o'clock on a Saturday morning?" Kate sighed. She'd been all over the library, and there was no sign of Sasha.

"Hey there," she heard Sasha call just as she was about to give up and go home. Sasha was walking in, wearing the familiar blue jacket and carrying her backpack, which seemed even more overstuffed than usual.

"What did you do, bring everything you own?" Kate joked.

"I have some stuff to do later," Sasha said. "It's easier than going back and forth. So, you ready to help me write a brilliant paper?"

"I'll do my best," Kate said. "Let's find a table."

They went to a table beneath one of the library's big windows, where the sun made a large pool of light around them. Taking their coats off, they sat down.

"Okay," said Kate. "Who are you doing your report on?"

"I thought I'd take your advice and do Nathaniel Hawthorne," Sasha said. "I read *The Scarlet Letter*. It was nothing like the movie, but it was good. I especially like all of the witch stuff. So I thought I would see what I could dig up on old Nate."

"That should be easy," Kate said. "He's one of the biggies. The library is sure to have a lot of materials."

"Just point me to them," Sasha said.

Kate took Sasha to one of the library's reference computers and showed her how to look up things. Sure enough, the collection had a large number of books about Nathaniel Hawthorne and his work.

"Why don't you go check some of those out?" Kate suggested. "See what looks good and bring it back. We can start from there. I've got some of my own work I can do while you're looking up books."

"Will do," Sasha said. "You're the best."

Kate left Sasha at the computer and went back to the table. She had her own paper to work on, and she figured she might as well get some of it finished while she waited for Sasha. She'd decided to write about Carson McCullers, and had collected quite a bit of information about McCullers already so she was ready to outline her paper. She opened her notebook and started writing.

But she couldn't concentrate. She was still thinking about what had happened with Tyler on Thursday night. She couldn't believe that she'd pulled away from him like that. What had she been thinking? She'd wanted him to kiss her. But she had to admit that something had stopped her. Was it some kind of leftover feeling for Scott? She had barely even seen him since their breakup. Once he had come by her locker, but he just said hello and then walked away. She had tried to call him a couple of times, but every time she hung up before anyone answered, and she'd deleted all the e-mails she'd written him before they were even sent.

And why should she still have feelings for him anyway? She'd decided to be all independent and ask Tyler out, hadn't she? If Scott thought they were better off apart, she wasn't going to cry over it. She didn't want to be the kind of girl who sat around waiting for some guy to realize how great she was and come back to her. At least, she didn't think she did. But there was no reason for her not to kiss Tyler, and she still hadn't done it. When she'd looked at the rock where she and Scott sat the night they broke up, something inside of her had frozen. She just couldn't let herself be with Tyler. Something was going on. But what?

As she sat there alternating between thinking about her paper and thinking about her love life, she remembered Annie's list of pros and cons. Maybe if she made another one it would help her figure out what she was really feeling. Perhaps writing out her feelings about wanting to kiss Tyler and not wanting to kiss Tyler would make everything a little more clear. Turning her notebook to a new page, she started to make two columns. But her pen had run out of ink, and all she could get out of it was a faint line.

"Perfect," she said, slamming the pen down on the table. Now what was she going to do? Then she spied Sasha's backpack resting on the floor by her chair. Surely, Sasha would have an extra pen in there.

Kate leaned over and picked up the backpack. It was surprisingly heavy. She sat it on her lap and unzipped it. Inside there were all kinds of clothes and papers, all bunched up and shoved in with no rhyme or reason. Sasha apparently kept just about everything she owned in the pack.

Kate stuck her hand in and rummaged around,

looking for a pen. As she pushed her hand deeper inside, she felt a thick book in the way. She pulled it out so that she could see what was underneath.

Kate was surprised to see that the book was *Spells and Charms for the Modern Witch*, the same book she had first found in the school library. But why did Sasha have a copy of it? Kate flipped open the front cover, and there she saw Annie's name written in her small, precise handwriting. Sasha had taken the book from Annie's room. That's why Annie had been unable to find it. But why? What would Sasha want with that book?

Kate opened the backpack again and searched further. As she rooted around in the bag, she felt a strangely shaped object beneath her fingers. Grabbing whatever it was, she pulled it out.

It was a doll. It looked like some kind of old Barbie, only its hair was brown instead of blond, and most of the paint had worn off its face. It was wearing a faded blue dress, and only one of its feet had a shoe on it. It looked like something that someone had thrown away and someone else had picked out of the garbage.

But that wasn't the strangest thing. Wrapped around the doll in a haphazard way was a red ribbon, circling the doll's body from its feet to its neck. When Kate saw it, her blood ran cold. It looked just like the doll she had made when she'd tried to get Scott to fall in love with her using magic.

Only this was a girl doll. Kate wasn't sure who

it was supposed to represent, but she knew what it was for, and that was bad enough. Sasha was trying to do a spell. But for what? And involving who? Kate didn't know. But she knew that bound to the doll by the ribbon there would be a paper heart. Kate also knew that there would be a name written on the heart—the name of the person Sasha was trying to make fall in love with whomever the doll represented. She just wasn't sure she wanted to see whose name it was. Something about the doll made her terribly afraid.

But she knew that she had to look. Moving apart some of the red ribbon, she found the edge of the paper heart and pulled. The paper came away easily, slipping out from underneath the ribbon. Sasha had used plain old notebook paper instead of red construction paper, but she had still cut it out in the correct shape. Kate unfolded the heart and forced herself to look at it. Scott's name was written there in blue pen.

Kate knew then who the doll was supposed to be. It was Sasha. She was trying to use the "Come to Me Love Spell" to get Scott to fall for her.

But why? Kate wondered. Why would Sasha do such a thing? She knew all about Kate's own ill-fated attempt at doing the spell. Why would she try it herself? And why would she try to do it to Kate's boyfriend?

Ex-boyfriend, a voice in Kate's head reminded her. Scott had dumped her.

Almost immediately, Kate started to think. When had the book disappeared from Annie's room? She counted back. Annie had noticed it was missing on Friday, but Sasha had been in the house on Wednesday. And she had rushed out very suddenly. Had she taken the book then? She must have.

Kate thought some more. Scott had broken up with her on Friday night. That was two days after Sasha stole the book. It didn't take Kate long to do the math and come to a conclusion. *She must have done the spell on Wednesday or Thursday*, Kate thought. *That's why Scott acted so cold. That's why we broke up!*

That still didn't answer the question of why Sasha had done it at all. Had she wanted Scott to break up with Kate? Apparently so. But she had seemed so friendly, and Kate was going out of her way to help her with her paper. Why would Sasha want to do that to someone who had only been her friend? Kate didn't understand.

"I found some stuff," she heard Sasha say, and looked up. Sasha was walking towards her, her arms filled with books. "I couldn't decide which ones were the best, so I brought them all. We can—"

She stopped talking when she saw Kate holding the doll in her hand.

"What is this?" Kate asked, holding up the doll in one hand and the heart with Scott's name written on it in the other. "What are you doing?"

Sasha dropped the books on the table. She

opened her mouth to say something, then stopped. Finally she spoke. "What were you doing looking in my bag?" she asked angrily.

"I was looking for a pen," Kate said. "Now, tell me what this stuff is."

"I was just fooling around," Sasha said, not looking at Kate. "You had talked about your spell, and it sounded sort of cool. I was just playing around, that's all."

"This is supposed to be you, isn't it?" Kate said, her voice even and flat.

Sasha didn't answer her.

"Isn't it?" Kate said, a little more loudly.

Sasha looked around. "Not so loud, okay? Yes, it's supposed to be me."

"And you were trying to get my boyfriend to fall in love with you," Kate continued. "Why? Why would you do that?"

Sasha shrugged. "Why did *you* do it?" she said. "For fun, I guess. To see if I could. I don't know."

"You don't know?" said Kate. "What do you mean you don't know? You just thought it would be fun to see if you could get him to break up with me?"

"I didn't know that was going to happen!" Sasha said. "I didn't know what would happen. It's not my fault my spell worked when yours didn't."

"Yeah, well, yours doesn't seem to have worked, either," Kate said with venom in her voice. "I don't see Scott with you."

She and Sasha stared at one another. Kate felt

like throwing the doll at her. Her whole body was shaking with anger.

"Haven't you been listening at all in class?" she said. "Or to what Annie, Cooper, and I have been saying? This isn't what magic is for. You've really screwed things up."

"I don't know why you're so upset," Sasha said. "Cooper and Annie didn't think Scott was good enough for you anyway. And now you've got Tyler."

"I suppose you did some spell to make him fall for me," Kate said bitterly.

Sasha gave a short laugh. "No, you did that all by yourself," she said. "And you didn't seem to waste any time doing it, either."

"What's that supposed to mean?" Kate asked.

"It means that if you thought Scott was so great, why did you let him go so easily?" Sasha shot back.

Kate didn't have an answer for her. This only made her madder. She just sat there, glaring at Sasha and wishing there was something she could do to hurt her, to make her feel the way Kate was feeling inside—miserable and frustrated.

"You have everything," Sasha said suddenly. "Great friends. A great family. And *two* guys interested in you. What difference does it make if I have one of them?"

Kate was dumbstruck. She couldn't believe what Sasha was saying. "You mean you did this because you're jealous of me?" she said.

Sasha bit her lip. Her chin trembled as if she was

trying hard not to cry. A tear slipped from her eye and she wiped it away quickly, before it ran down her cheek.

"I just wanted to be a little bit like you," Sasha said. "I thought maybe this would do it."

Kate was still furious, but she calmed down a little bit as she watched Sasha trying to control herself. She motioned for Sasha to come sit next to her, and the other girl slumped into a chair.

"You can't be like someone else by taking what she has," Kate said. "You have to be who you are all on your own."

"The spell seemed so easy," Sasha said. "I remembered everything you said, and I tried to do it right. And really, at first I just did it to see if I could make it work where you didn't. That's why I used a doll that looked like me, instead of one that looked like Scott, the way you did. I thought that might be what you did wrong. I was going to surprise you and show you that I could do it right."

"Some surprise," Kate said, trying to make sense of Sasha's story. "Taking my boyfriend away isn't the best surprise I can think of. Did you really think I'd be *happy* that you did it?"

"It wasn't supposed to go that far," Sasha said. "I just wanted Scott to pay some attention to me. Then I was going to reverse the spell, once you all saw that I could pull it off. I didn't think you'd actually break up."

Kate sighed. "Why not?" she said. "That spell has a mind of its own. Maybe he really only did like me in the first place because I did it, and then when you did it the magic decided that my fun was over. Maybe this was supposed to happen."

Sasha wiped her eyes and grabbed Kate's hand. "Oh, Kate," she said. "I really am sorry. I didn't mean for anything really bad to happen. You have to believe me."

Kate looked at her. "In a strange way, I do believe you," she said. "I didn't mean to cause any trouble when I did the spell either." She was thinking about Terri Fletcher, the girl Scott was supposed to go to the Valentine's Day dance with before Kate did the spell that made him ask her instead. Terri had been devastated when Scott broke their date. But at the time, Kate hadn't cared. She'd only been interested in getting Scott for herself.

"Is there anything I can do to make it up to you?" Sasha asked. "Really, I'll do whatever I can."

"You can start by getting rid of this," Kate said, waving the doll at her. "That might help. But I don't think you can do anything to change what's happened between me and Scott. More and more, I think this is what was supposed to happen. You just helped it along a little."

Sasha took the doll from Kate. Taking one end of the ribbon, she unwound it and crumpled the length of ribbon in her hand. "There," she said. "That's that."

"It's not that easy," Kate said. "Believe me. But it's a start."

Sasha gave a weak smile and put the doll back into her backpack. "I'll work on the rest later," she said. "Can you forgive me?"

"It won't do me much good to be mad," Kate said. "But promise me one thing?"

"Anything," Sasha said.

"Keep your hands off my Ken doll when you come to my house."

chapter 11

"She did *what?*" Cooper exploded.

Kate was standing at her locker with Annie and Cooper on Monday morning. She'd just finished telling them about what Sasha had done with the doll.

"I can't believe you waited this long to tell us," Cooper said. "And I can't believe you didn't wring her neck."

"What would be the point?" Kate sighed. "It wouldn't change anything."

"You're taking this awfully well," Annie said. "What gives?"

Kate leaned against her locker. "I don't know," she said. "I mean, I *was* really angry at her when I found out. But I don't think she did it to be malicious. And there's a part of me that thinks maybe this would have happened anyway."

"I think you're nuts," Cooper said. "I told you guys there was something weird about that girl."

"No, you didn't," Annie reminded her friend. "Kate did."

Cooper chewed her gum sullenly. "Well, I thought it," she said. "I just didn't want to be mean."

The other two rolled their eyes at her. Kate picked up her backpack and they started walking to class.

"Don't say anything to Sasha, okay?" Kate said. "I told her I wouldn't tell you guys and make a big deal out of this."

"It's going to be kind of hard to pretend we don't know," Annie said.

"Well, try," Kate said. "Starting now. Here she comes."

Sasha came jogging towards them, her backpack swinging from her arm. "Hey, guys," she said.

"Hey," Annie said. Cooper just nodded.

"Thanks again for helping me with my paper on Saturday, Kate," Sasha said. "It really helped."

"No problem," Kate said, trying to sound normal but feeling anything but.

"I've got to run," Sasha said. "But I'll catch you guys later."

As Sasha ran off, Sherrie, Jessica, and Tara appeared from around the corner.

"Graces alert," Cooper said. "This is my cue to leave."

"I'm right behind you," Annie said. "Later, Kate."

Kate waved good-bye as one set of her friends

left and the other arrived, like trains passing in a station.

"Kate," Sherrie said eagerly, "we've got to talk to you."

Kate knew that something must be up, because Sherrie hadn't made any nasty comments about Cooper and Annie, as she always did when she saw them.

"What's up?" Kate asked.

"Just the biggest piece of news ever," Tara said.

"Excuse me," Sherrie said, holding up her hand. "This is *my* moment here."

Tara backed off, and Sherrie turned to Kate again. "Guess what I saw last night?" she asked.

Kate shook her head. "I have no idea," she answered. "Ricky Martin having dinner at the Crab Pot?"

"Better," Jessica said, unable to contain her excitement.

"Sasha," Tara added impulsively.

Sherrie shot them both looks that made them put their hands over their mouths, silently promising to not say another word.

"Sasha and Ricky Martin at the Crab Pot?" Kate said, joking. "Come on, guys. What's the big deal about seeing Sasha?"

"It wasn't just Sasha," Sherrie said, clearly leading up to her big announcement. "It was Sasha and Scott."

"Your Scott," Jessica added, as if Kate didn't

know who Sherrie meant.

"You saw Sasha and Scott together?" Kate said, bewildered. "Last night?"

Sherrie nodded. "They were at the Frozen Cow, sitting at one of the tables in the back. I walked by and saw them. They looked awfully cozy. Sasha was laughing a lot, and Scott seemed *very* interested in whatever it was she had to say to him."

"And you're sure it was them?" Kate pressed.

"Please," said Sherrie, sounding offended. "It's not like there's that many big, blue-eyed football players and little skinny girls in blue jackets running around town. Yes, it was them."

Kate didn't know what to say. She couldn't believe that after everything that had happened, Sasha would go out with Scott. She'd seemed so sincere about how sorry she was for causing the trouble between him and Kate. But then she had turned around and gone on a *date* with him?

"Cooper was right," Kate said. "She is trouble."

"What was that?" Sherrie asked.

Kate looked up, remembering where she was and who she was talking to. "Nothing," she said. "Look, guys, thanks for telling me about this. I've got to go."

Kate turned and ran down the hall. Sherrie called out for her to come back, but Kate knew that she had to do what she needed to do right away, before she changed her mind. She raced up the stairs and headed for the chemistry lab.

Sasha was sitting in her seat a few rows behind Kate's seat. She had her notebook open, and she was reading over some notes. Kate walked up to her and stood with her arms crossed, her heart beating and her body almost shaking.

"Hey," Sasha said, looking up.

"Did you have fun on your date with Scott last night?" Kate hissed.

Sasha's face fell, and she looked frightened. "Kate, wait. I can explain that," she said.

"Right," Kate snapped. "Just like you could explain the doll in your backpack with that stupid story about just wanting to fit in. I bet you were really proud of yourself, having me all fooled into feeling sorry for you."

"It wasn't a story," Sasha said. "If you would just let me tell you what I was doing."

"Don't bother," Kate snapped. "Just listen, and listen good. I was willing to give you a second chance after what you did. I believed you when you said you didn't mean to cause any trouble. And then, as soon as I'm gone, you start going out with Scott."

"Kate—" Sasha began.

"Forget it," Kate said, cutting her off. "I'm through with you. You were right—you can't fix what you did. But you can stay out of my way. And I suggest you do."

She turned and stormed over to her seat. The bell had just rung, and students were pouring into the room. Annie walked by Kate on her way to her seat in the next row.

"What did the Graces do to put that look on your face?" she asked.

"It wasn't them," Kate said sharply. "It was Sasha. I'll tell you later."

Kate didn't hear a thing Miss Blackwood said during class. She was too angry to listen. All she could think about was how Sasha had tricked her and how stupid she'd been for thinking that maybe everything with Scott had really been an accident— or even her own fault. Now she knew the truth, and she wasn't going to be fooled again.

After class Kate left quickly, before Sasha could try to talk to her and tell her any more lies. Annie ran after her, jogging to keep up with Kate's furious pace. As she stormed through the halls, Kate told Annie about Sasha and Scott.

"You're sure Sherrie isn't just making it up?" Annie asked.

Kate shook her head. "Sherrie's a gossip," she answered. "But she doesn't make things up. I have to give her that much. Besides, after what happened with the doll, it all makes perfect sense. Sasha had this planned all along. She'd probably been waiting for the perfect moment ever since I told her about the spell I did in the first place."

"What are you going to do?" Annie asked.

"Nothing," Kate said. "I'm not going to do a thing. If Sasha really is playing around with spells, she's going to get hers in the end, the same way I did. It won't do me any good to try to make things right. Until then, I'm just going to ignore her."

For two days, that's exactly what Kate did. She barely saw Sasha all day Monday or Tuesday. Even when they had classes together, she made sure she never looked at Sasha or acknowledged her. She just pretended that Sasha wasn't there. Sasha seemed to get the hint. She didn't try to sit with Kate, Sherrie, Tara, and Jessica at lunch, and she stayed away from Cooper and Annie as well. The few times Kate actually caught a glimpse of her, she seemed miserable, which made Kate feel satisfied. If she had to be unhappy, she wanted Sasha to suffer too.

It wasn't until Tuesday night, when they all went to Crones' Circle for their final class, that she had to be in close proximity to the girl she now considered her biggest enemy. She was almost surprised that Sasha even showed up. She'd expected her to be too ashamed to show her face.

"This is our final class," Rowan reminded them as class began. "Next week, for those who choose to participate, we'll be holding the dedication ceremony. I won't ask you until the end of class tonight if you want to take part in that or not. First we're going to talk about our last topic. One of the things that is very important to many witches is community—the people we do rituals and magic with. A coven is a community. So are our friends and families. Even solitaries—witches who practice by themselves without being in a coven—generally have other people they talk to about magical things, whether they're friends or people they communicate with online. Take a moment and think about what kind of community you have around yourselves."

Kate put her arms around her knees and hugged them to her chest as she thought. What kind of community was she a part of? Who were the members? Cooper and Annie definitely counted, especially when it came to Wicca. But what about Sherrie, Jessica, and Tara? She wasn't as close to them as she used to be, but they still played a part in her life, although in a different way. Then there was her family—and the people at Crones' Circle. All of these different groups made up her community. Yet they weren't all part of each other's communities. Her family didn't know anything about her involvement in witchcraft. Her friends didn't all like one another. She sometimes felt pulled in too many directions.

As she thought about all these things, Kate's gaze wandered around the room, and she caught a glimpse of Sasha, who was sitting as far away from Kate, Annie, and Cooper as possible. Sasha had been part of her community for a while. But she had turned out not to be any kind of friend at all, and Kate definitely didn't want her as part of her community. But was she part of it anyway, simply because she was in the class and attended the same school?

Kate looked away, and she saw Tyler sitting in a chair by the door. She'd avoided him when she came in because she didn't know what to say about what had happened on their date. But could she avoid him forever? He was definitely part of the same community she was. How was she going to deal with that?

"Okay," Rowan said. "You've had a little time to think about what community means to you personally. Now we're going to do a little exercise to show just how important that community can be. I want you all to join up with the small groups you've been working with for the past two classes."

Kate groaned. The last two people she wanted to face right now were Sasha and Tyler, and she was going to be in a group with them. But she knew it would look strange if she tried to get out of it, so she stood up and reluctantly wandered over to where they were clustered around Lea.

"There are times when you're going to need to count on the support of the community you create," Rowan said when everyone was organized. "To illustrate this point, we're going to do a trust exercise. Three of your group members are going to stand together. The fourth is going to stand in front of you with her or his back to the group. That person will then fall backward. It's the job of the other three to make sure that fourth person doesn't hit the floor. And don't worry—you'll each get a chance to fall."

There was nervous laughter from the class members as they decided who in their groups would be the first one to fall. Kate looked around at the others, hoping one of them would volunteer. Finally Lea stepped forward.

"Just remember," she said as she got into position. "These old bones aren't as strong as they used to be."

Kate stood beside Tyler, keeping Sasha as far away as possible. They held out their hands and waited for Lea to tumble backward. Lea took a deep breath, then let herself go. Her body fell toward the waiting hands, and then she was in their arms, supported gently on a web of fingers.

Tyler was the next to go, followed by Sasha. As she watched Sasha begin to fall, Kate was tempted to not catch her, to let her crash to the floor in a heap. It was what she deserved. But at the last second, she instinctively reached out and added her hands to those of Lea and Tyler, and Sasha was lifted safely up.

Then it was her turn. It had been pretty easy to catch the others. But when Kate found herself standing with her back to them, unable to see anything, it was a different story. She had to trust that they would reach out and stop her from hitting the floor. But did she trust them? She had no reason to trust Sasha. And for all she knew, Tyler was angry with her for running off after their date. Now she was supposed to count on them.

She closed her eyes. She knew they were all waiting for her. But she could refuse to do the exercise. She could just walk away and forget the whole thing.

Before she gave in to the temptation to back out, she fell. It seemed as if everything moved in slow motion. She felt herself flying through the air. Once she started, she knew she couldn't stop, although she very badly wanted to. It seemed like she was falling forever. They weren't catching her. She waited for her body to smack against the hard floor, and she steeled herself for the impact.

But then she was reclining against outstretched hands. They had stopped her after all. As she felt her teammates lift her back to a standing position, she was filled with a peculiar sense of relief and joy. They hadn't let her fall. Even Sasha had reached out to help her.

"Now you have some idea of what being part of a community can feel like," Rowan said. "In falling, you had to trust that there would be people there to stop you from getting hurt. Some of those people might have been strangers to you. Others might have been people you didn't exactly like. But you had to trust them. You also had to trust yourself. And that's what deciding to take part in the dedication ritual is all about. You have to believe, first, that studying Wicca is what's right for you and that you are willing to set out on an adventure, even when it might be scary or hard. Second, you have to trust the people in the community you'll be becoming a part of, because you're going to need them, and they're going to need you. If you think you can do those things, then I invite you to take the first step. Anya and I will be here taking the names of those who want to participate in next week's ritual."

The groups broke up and people began going up to talk to the two women. Kate looked around for Annie and Cooper. They were already in line, where she joined them.

"Are you in?" Cooper asked.

"I'm in," Kate said. "Do you think I'd let you two do this without me?"

When it was their turn, Rowan smiled at them. "I had a feeling you three would be joining us," she said as she wrote down their names. "Here's a list of things you'll need to know for the ritual. My number is on there as well, so you can call if you have any questions."

The girls took the information sheets and went to look them over. As they were perusing them, Kate noticed Sasha going up to Rowan. A minute later she was standing beside Kate, her face red and angry.

"What did you tell them about me?" she demanded.

"What are you talking about?" Cooper said as

Kate looked at Sasha, confused.

"She told them something about me," Sasha said. "Rowan just told me they don't think I'm ready for the dedication ceremony. I want to know what Kate said to her."

"Nothing," Kate said defensively. "Why would I say anything about you?"

Sasha glared at her, not saying anything. When she finally spoke, she sounded like she might cry. "You don't think I can be a real witch," she said. "Well, just watch out."

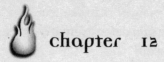

chapter 12

Kate was really looking forward to lunch the next day. She wanted to tell Sherrie she had been right about Sasha. More important, she wanted her friends to be as angry at Sasha as she was. She knew that they were already suspicious of her because of what had happened with Scott, but she hoped to make sure once and for all that they knew how conniving she was. She couldn't believe that Sasha was blaming her for the fact that Rowan and the others thought she wasn't ready for the ritual. *She* was the one who was causing trouble. As Kate walked into the cafeteria, she imagined all of the catty things Sherrie would have to say. For once, she was anxious to hear them.

But her joy faded when she saw that Sasha was already sitting with Tara, Sherrie, and Jessica at their regular table. Even worse, they seemed to be *happy* that she was with them. What was she doing there? She knew that Kate ate lunch with her friends almost every day. Why would she willingly put herself in a position where she'd be facing their ridicule? And why would her friends welcome someone who had done what Sasha had done? Seeing Sasha sitting in what was usually her seat made Kate even madder than she'd been when she'd confronted Sasha about seeing Scott. She started to charge over, already forming her words in her mind.

Then she hesitated. Maybe she shouldn't eat lunch with her friends. Maybe she should go somewhere else. If they wanted to side with Sasha, she didn't want to give Sasha the chance to rub it in her face. But where else could she go? She couldn't sit with Scott and his friends. Annie had gone to the library to look up some materials for one of her classes. And Cooper was probably hanging out in the music rooms with some of her other friends, the ones who thought girls like Kate were a little too clean-cut to talk to.

Besides, she wasn't about to let Sasha scare her away. If she wanted to play games, Kate was willing to play them too. Sasha might have taken Kate's boyfriend, but Kate wasn't about to give up this round so easily. Taking a deep breath, she walked over to her friends' table and sat down next to Jessica.

"Hey," she said, as if nothing was wrong.

"Hey," Tara said. "We were just talking about you. Well, sort of."

"Really?" Kate said. "Anything interesting?"

"Sasha was just telling us how she ran into Scott the other night," Sherrie said. "At the Frozen Cow."

"Did she?" said Kate, trying to sound disinterested as she gave Sherrie a look and her friend raised her eyebrows in response.

"I was there with my parents," Sasha said, not speaking directly to Kate but making sure Kate was listening. "Scott was there with someone else. A girl I didn't recognize."

"I can't imagine who that might have been," Sherrie said. "What did she look like?"

"You know," Sasha replied. "A girl. Blond. Kind of pretty."

"Sounds like Terri Fletcher," Jessica said.

"I don't know," Sasha said. "Anyway, I was going to just ignore him, but he said hello to me, and I figured I had to say something back."

"Of course," said Sherrie, feigning sincerity.

"That was really it," Sasha said. "I just thought it was interesting that he was there with that girl, that's all. I'm going to go get a soda. Does anyone want one?"

No one did. When Sasha was out of earshot, Kate turned to Sherrie. "Of course she's lying," she said. "She said all that just so I would hear it and believe her."

"Maybe," said Sherrie.

"What do you mean maybe?" Kate asked. "You said yourself that you saw Sasha talking to Scott. Not some blond girl—Sasha."

"Well, she *was* talking to him," Sherrie said. "But there might have been someone else there too. I didn't get *that* close a look. Maybe the other girl was in the bathroom."

Kate groaned. "Come on," she said. "You don't really believe that she just happened to run into him, do you?"

"It is possible," Jessica said. "I mean, that makes more sense than Scott's being there with Sasha. Why would he be there with her?"

Because she put a spell on him! Kate wanted to scream. But she knew she couldn't say that. For one thing, her friends would never believe that something like magic was real. For another, it would mean explaining to them how she knew anything about how spells worked. She had to find some other way to make them see what Sasha was doing.

"Look, Kate," Tara said before Kate could think of something to say. "We all know that you're upset about Scott. He dumped you. We'd all be upset too. And Sherrie didn't help things by not getting all the facts straight."

Sherrie started to speak, but for once Tara cut her off. "Not that it was her fault or anything. The point is—you know Scott would never go for someone like Sasha, so probably she's telling the truth."

"You didn't think he would ever go for me, either," Kate reminded her. "In fact, you were positive he would never ask me out, remember?"

"Good point," Tara countered. "But that was different."

"How?" Kate demanded.

"It just was," Sherrie said, unable to contain herself any longer. "Sasha just isn't the kind of girl who can steal other girls' boyfriends. She's too rough around the edges."

"You're being pretty protective of someone you were ready to write off a few days ago," Kate said.

"I know," Sherrie said. "But she kind of grows on you. And you know I'm always the first one to admit when I'm wrong about something."

That was the problem—Kate knew Sherrie would *never* admit when she was wrong. That's what made her sudden change of heart about Sasha even more confusing. Something else was going on. Her friends were trying to convince her that the girl who had stolen her boyfriend hadn't really done it. Ordinarily they would be ripping Sasha apart in defense of Kate.

Maybe it's another spell, Kate thought suddenly. *Maybe she did some kind of spell to make my friends like her.* Why not? It made sense. First Sasha had done the spell to steal Scott away, and then she'd tried to cover it up. But what if she and Scott really *had* been on a date when Sherrie saw them? What if Sasha had just been trying to throw Kate off the trail when she'd said all that stuff about not really understanding what the spell would do? What if she really *did* know exactly what she was doing and was just trying to cover her tracks again now? If she had done some kind of spell involving Sherrie, Tara, and Jessica, maybe they weren't able to see things clearly.

But that's insane, Kate told herself. She had herself tied up in knots trying to figure out what Sasha was up to. She didn't know what to believe or what to think. Plus, she wanted her friends to side with her, and they weren't. She felt as if they were slipping away from her, falling more and more under Sasha's spell. But she couldn't tell them anything about Sasha's involvement with witchcraft because it would mean exposing herself too.

She saw Sasha coming back to the table carrying her soda, and she knew she couldn't stand to listen to her telling any more lies. Getting up, she stuffed what was left of her sandwich into her bag.

"I forgot," she said. "I have something I need to do."

She left quickly, not looking back. She knew that they would talk about her after she was gone, and she didn't want to see them doing it. She didn't want to see what were supposed to be her friends laughing at Sasha's jokes or including her in their plans. She needed to talk to someone she knew would take her side.

She found Cooper in one of the practice rooms, just as she'd expected. She was playing her guitar, and a guy wearing a faded Blink 182 T-shirt and pants cut off just below the knees was standing across from her, a battered bass guitar in his hands. Cooper was nodding as the guy plucked out a sequence of notes. When she heard the door to the room open, she looked up.

"Kate," she said, sounding surprised. "What are you doing here?"

"Can I talk to you?" she asked.

Cooper put down her guitar. "Kate, this is T.J. We write songs together sometimes."

T.J. nodded at Kate. He was a tall, thin boy whose reddish hair had been shaved almost down to the skin. There were three gold rings in one ear and a stud in his nose. Kate had seen him around school, but she had never seen him with Cooper. Then again, she'd never really met *any* of Cooper's friends.

T.J. looked at Cooper. "We can do this some other time," he said. "If you guys need to talk. It's cool with me."

"Thanks," Cooper said. "I'll call you tonight. Maybe we can work on the lyrics some more. It's really coming together now, and I like that line you laid down."

T.J. put his bass into its case and locked it. As he walked out, he reached out and slapped Cooper's outstretched hand, their fingers touching for an instant. "Later," he said.

"Something I should know?" Kate asked when T.J. was gone, her need to talk about her own problems momentarily eclipsed by her curiosity about Cooper's relationship with a guy she'd never even mentioned to Annie and Kate.

"No," Cooper said flatly. "You're the one who ventured down here into the Underworld, not me. I don't have to answer any questions."

Kate thought about pressing her friend for more information. Of all her friends, she knew the least about Cooper's life away from the group. Cooper never talked about what she did when she wasn't with Annie and Kate, and Kate sometimes wondered about her life outside of school. But Cooper had a look on her face that warned Kate that asking about T.J. was definitely off-limits for the time being. Besides, she was right. Kate *had* come to talk to her.

"It's Sasha," she said. "I think she's up to something."

"There's a news flash," Cooper said. "Didn't

you kind of get that feeling when she made your boyfriend disappear? And let's not forget her little performance last night."

"I know," Kate said. "But now she's getting all friendly with Sherrie and the girls. It's like she's trying to take over my life."

"Maybe she is," Cooper said. "Didn't she say that she was jealous of you when you confronted her about the doll?"

Kate nodded. "Yes," she said. "She said that she was jealous because I had everything she wanted." She thought about telling Cooper Sasha's latest excuse about why she'd been talking to Scott, but she didn't. It was obviously a lie, and anyway, she didn't want Cooper trying to convince her that Sasha might be telling the truth.

Cooper hoisted herself onto an amplifier. "So, first she went after your boyfriend. Maybe now she's trying to get to the Graces, although I don't know why she would want them. If she really wanted some cool friends, she'd try to get Annie and me on her side. Why that bunch of spritz-heads?"

"Because they're popular," Kate said. All of a sudden, everything made sense to her. Sasha *was* jealous of Kate. But it wasn't just about having a boyfriend. She wanted to be popular. Why hadn't she seen that before? "She thinks that if she has what I have, she'll be popular. That's why she wanted Scott, and that's why she wants to be friends with Jess, Tara, and Sherrie. She thinks if she can get everything that I had, she'll be happy."

"And she'll get revenge on you for ruining her bid for witchdom," Cooper added. "You have to admit, it's a plan."

"I have to stop her," Kate said, her mind racing as she tried to think of a plan of attack. "I can't let her do this to me. Maybe I can cast a spell back at her."

"Whoa," Cooper said. "Listen to yourself. Don't you remember what Anya said about revenge spells? They just make things worse."

"But I can't just let her get away with all of this!" Kate wailed. "It's not fair!"

"I didn't say you shouldn't do anything," Cooper said. "I just said you shouldn't try to get even. Maybe there's something about Sasha we don't know."

"Like that she's a demon from the pit of hell?" Kate suggested hopefully.

"It's a thought," Cooper admitted. "But not likely. All I'm saying is that maybe you should think of a positive approach to this instead of trying to zap her with whatever she's zapping you with."

"You're the one who's supposed to have the wild streak," Kate said. "What gives?"

"Maybe you're rubbing off on me," Cooper said, grinning.

* * *

That night, Kate sat in her bedroom surrounded by a circle of white candles. Taking a deep breath, she tried to envision herself sitting in a peaceful grove of trees with a full moon overhead filling the grove with light. It was a meditation she did whenever she was stressed out. And she was definitely stressed out.

It took her a while, but eventually she felt herself calming down as she imagined roots going from her body down into the ground until they reached a pool of warm, golden light. She breathed deeply, drawing that light up into herself, letting it fill her with its warmth.

When she felt filled with light, she pictured Sasha standing in front of her. Sasha had an angry expression on her face. Kate reached out to her, letting the golden light within her body flow out through her hands and surround Sasha. At first she could only manage to see Sasha with a faint yellow haze around her body. But with a little concentration she was able to imagine the two of them surrounded by a cocoon of gold, their bodies seeming to float within the healing light.

She imagined all of the anger she had toward Sasha within herself burning away in the light and being replaced with peacefulness. She tried too, to imagine the negative feelings in Sasha being replaced with ones of happiness. For a moment, it seemed to be working.

Then, just as suddenly as it had appeared, the

image of Sasha faded. Kate waited a minute, then opened one eye and looked around the room. Why had the vision ended so quickly? And had it worked? She let herself relax for a moment. She definitely felt a little calmer.

But I still don't like her, she thought to herself. Apparently, doing magic to get over being mad at someone wasn't as easy as it seemed. She sighed heavily and blew out the candles around her.

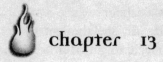

chapter 13

"I thought maybe you wouldn't talk to me," Scott said.

Kate gripped the telephone tightly, half afraid that if she let go of it Scott would disappear, as if only her hand holding on to the receiver was keeping him on the other end. When she'd heard the phone ringing and picked it up, she'd expected to hear her father's voice telling her when he'd be home from the store. When she'd heard Scott's voice instead, she'd been tempted to hang up. But she hadn't been able to. Now she stood in the kitchen, unable to think of anything to say to him.

"I was wondering if you would meet me," Scott said. "So we can talk."

"I don't know," Kate said, suddenly finding her voice and remembering that she was talking to the guy who had dumped her without warning. "Is there anything to talk about?"

"I think there is," Scott answered. "But I don't want to do it on the phone. I was hoping we could take a walk on the beach. I'll come pick you up."

"No," Kate said. "I'll take the bus." She didn't want to be in the car with Scott. She didn't know what he had to say, and if it was going to make her angry—or, worse, make her cry—she'd prefer to do it in front of strangers on the bus.

"Okay," Scott said. "Half an hour?"

"Fine," Kate said, and hung up.

As she pulled on a sweater and jeans, she tried to imagine what Scott could possibly have to say to her. They'd barely exchanged three words since the breakup. Why did he have to see her now? And why couldn't he just talk to her on the phone? Was he going to admit that he had gone out with Sasha? She still didn't know what to think about that. Despite the ritual she'd done the night before, she still couldn't bring herself to feel even the tiniest bit sorry for Sasha. Every time she tried, the girl did something else to make her angry. Just that afternoon Kate had seen her talking to Sherrie as they walked to class. They were laughing like old friends. Meanwhile, Kate was feeling more and more like the outsider as her friends seemed to be choosing Sasha over her.

She tried to not think about it as she walked to the bus stop and waited. But no matter how she tried, she couldn't get the image of Sasha out of her mind. In only a few weeks, the girl had managed to turn everything in Kate's life upside down. Kate wished that she had never even gone to the Spring

Equinox ritual. But then she would probably never have taken the class or decided to do the dedication ritual. *And you would never have met Tyler*, she thought unexpectedly.

Tyler. He was another problem. What was she going to do about him? She couldn't just keep ignoring him. But what was she going to say? She felt so stupid about not kissing him on the beach. What had she been thinking? If only Scott hadn't dumped her, she never would have gone out with Tyler in the first place. And if only Sasha hadn't done the spell, Scott wouldn't have broken up with her. Once again, it all came back to Sasha.

But she *had* gone out with Tyler. She couldn't take that back. And she'd really enjoyed herself. He was easy to talk to, and he actually listened to what she had to say. Scott sometimes seemed more interested in football than in Kate. And Tyler was cute, there was no denying it. *Maybe I should give him a second chance*, she thought. *That is, if he'll give* me *a second chance*. She wasn't entirely sure that he would. After all, she had acted pretty strangely on their date, and she'd avoided him since then. Probably he'd had enough. *But you won't know unless you try*, she told herself as the bus neared her stop. *But what do I do about Scott? Nothing but have this last talk* she decided. And by the time she got off fifteen minutes later, she'd decided to call Tyler that night and see if he wanted another date.

Scott was already standing on the beach when

she reached the bottom of the stairs. He was wearing old jeans and a sweatshirt with the hood thrown back. His back was to Kate as she walked toward him, and he didn't see her until she spoke.

"Hi," she said softly.

Scott turned around and smiled. "Hi," he said. "Thanks for coming."

"Well, it's not every day a girl gets asked to meet her ex-boyfriend for a secret rendezvous," Kate said. "How could I resist?" Her words sounded harsh, and Scott looked away from her for a moment, as if she'd slapped him.

"I just didn't want to talk on the phone," Scott replied.

"So you thought we should return to the scene of the crime?" Kate asked, her voice rising.

"You're not making this very easy," Scott said.

"Why should I?" Kate retorted. "You didn't make it very easy on me." All of a sudden, she didn't know why she'd even agreed to come. What was the point of even talking to Scott? It was over after all, and she'd started to get on with her life. Did she just want to make him feel bad? Did she want to tell him what she thought of him?

"I know," Scott said. "I know what I said came as a total surprise."

"That's an understatement," said Kate.

"Look," Scott said. "I've been thinking."

"That's how our last conversation started," Kate said, interrupting him. "Why don't I just leave now and we can skip the part in the middle where you dump me."

"Will you just let me finish?" Scott pleaded.

Kate didn't say anything, standing with her arms across her chest staring at Scott, as if daring him to say something else that was going to make her angry.

"I was talking with Sasha the other night," he said.

"Sasha!" Kate said, forgetting herself. "So you *did* go out with her!"

"Go out with her?" Scott said, as if that was the most ridiculous thing he'd ever heard. "No, I didn't go out with her. I ran into her at the Frozen Cow while I was there with Sheila Pruitt."

Kate looked at him with an expression of disbelief on her face. Seeing it, Scott hastily added, "And no, I wasn't on a date with Sheila, either. We were discussing the senior trip. We're on the planning committee."

Kate tried to process everything Scott was telling her, but there was too much going through her mind at once. "Wait a minute," she said. "You weren't on a date with Sasha, but you did talk to her?"

Scott nodded. Kate didn't know what to think. Sasha hadn't lied to her. She really had just run into Scott by accident. But that still didn't explain why she had talked to him at all.

"What did she say to you?" Kate asked. Part of

her suspected that Sasha had tried to ask Scott out, even if she hadn't been there with him in the first place.

"She wanted to talk about you," Scott said.

"Me?" said Kate. "What? She wanted to tell you that I had a date with someone else or something?" She'd mentioned the date thing before she could think not to. She hoped Scott would ignore it, but he didn't.

"You had a date with someone?" he asked, sounding hurt. "Who?"

"No one," Kate lied. "Just tell me what Sasha said about me. I'm sure it's another one of her lies anyway."

"I don't know," Scott said. "You tell me. She told me that breaking up with you was a big mistake because we seemed really great together. She said she wished we would try to work things out."

Kate felt as if she'd just woken up from a bad dream and didn't know where she was or what was going on. "She said that?" she asked, not believing it.

"Yes," Scott said. "But maybe you're right. Maybe she lied."

Kate didn't know how to respond. Sasha had told Scott that they made a good couple? That didn't make any sense if she was trying to break them up. For a minute she just stood there, the sea wind whipping her hair around her face.

"I don't know what to say," she said finally.

"I've been thinking about things since then,"

Scott told her. "And I think she's right. I think we have something special. Really special."

He took Kate's hand, and she didn't pull away. She'd forgotten how big Scott's hands were, and how nice it felt having him hold hers. For a moment it felt like before. But then she remembered why they had broken up in the first place.

"We can't be a couple," she said. "It doesn't make sense, what with you going off to school in New York and me being here."

"I know," Scott said. "That's why I told New York no and accepted the offer here."

Kate was speechless. Scott was grinning at her, but she wasn't sure she'd heard him correctly.

"You're staying?" she said. "Here?"

Scott nodded. "Well, not exactly here. The school is a couple of hours away. But that's a lot closer than New York. We can even see each other on weekends. That is, if you want to get back together."

Scott was staying. Kate couldn't believe it. He was staying, and he wanted to get back together with her. Why had he changed his mind? Had it been what Sasha said to him? Had her spell really ended? Kate didn't know. And at the moment, she didn't care. All she could think about was the fact that Scott wanted her back. Everything else she had been thinking about seemed unimportant.

"Yes," she said. "Yes!" she said again, more

loudly. "Yes, I want to get back together!"

Scott took her in his arms and spun her around. The sand and sky blurred together as she let herself enjoy the feeling of being held by him again. She hadn't realized just how much she missed him until that moment. But now it didn't matter. They were back together. She couldn't wait to tell the girls.

But who would she tell? Annie and Cooper would probably think she was crazy. No, she *knew* they would think she was crazy. Sherrie and the others might be happy for her, but telling them would mean having to admit that she had been wrong about Sasha.

Sasha. Her stomach sank as she thought about Sasha. Kate had accused her of being a traitor, and she'd been wrong. Sasha had been trying to help her. Kate felt ashamed as she recalled how she had told Sasha off in the chemistry lab and how she'd been wishing that something bad would happen to her. No wonder Sasha thought that Kate had something to do with her being told she couldn't participate in the dedication ritual. But that really hadn't had anything to do with Kate.

She had to let Sasha know that. And she had to apologize for the way she'd treated her. Her mind flashed back to lunch the day before, when Sasha had been trying to explain about meeting Scott at the Frozen Cow. But Kate had run off before she could get the full story. She had made assumptions that weren't true, and she had hurt someone's feelings in the process. Sasha might be impulsive and immature sometimes, but Kate had judged her too quickly.

I'll make it up to her, Kate thought as Scott put her down again. *I don't know how, but I'll find a way.*

chapter 14

The Summer House, where Sasha had said she worked, didn't look anything like its name suggested. It was an ugly cinder block building that had been painted a sickly shade of green in an attempt to brighten it up. But nothing could hide the graffiti spray painted on the walls or the trash that littered the sidewalk around the building's doors. A mural, long faded, depicted a field of sunflowers along one wall, but it did nothing to dispel the atmosphere of gloom that surrounded the place.

Kate crossed the street and pushed open the door. It had taken her a while to find the right address, and it had been a much longer walk than she'd anticipated. She was relieved to finally be there, even if the condition of the building was something of a shock. But the building wasn't what she was there for. If she could just get the information she was after, she'd be all set.

She had intended to apologize to Sasha first thing Friday morning. But Sasha hadn't come to school. Kate asked Sherrie and the others if any of them knew where she was, but they didn't. Nor did any of them have Sasha's phone number. That's when Kate realized that Sasha had never given a number to anyone. She'd never told anyone where she lived, either. She always met up with them at someone else's house or at school.

Then Kate remembered the Summer House. She knew that Sasha spent a lot of time there doing volunteer work. Maybe, Kate thought, the people there would know how to reach her. She didn't want another day to go by with Sasha feeling responsible for what had happened between them. So after school, Kate had looked up the address of the shelter and walked there.

The inside of the Summer House wasn't much nicer than the outside. A stained, yellowing carpet covered the floor, and the cream-colored walls showed what looked to be many years' worth of dirt. Fingerprints, scuff marks, and other blemishes covered the surfaces, giving the place a tired, worn-out look. Looking at it all made Kate feel very sad, and she wanted to get away as quickly as she could.

There was what seemed to be a reception desk in one corner, with a bored-looking woman sitting behind it. She was reading a magazine, and she didn't look up when Kate came over to her.

"Excuse me," Kate said. "I need some help."

"Are you here for a bed?" the woman asked, barely glancing up. "Because we're all filled up.

Check-in time is six. After that, you're on your own."

"No," Kate said, a little offended that the woman would think she was a runaway. "I don't need a bed. I'm looking for a friend of mine."

"Is she registered with us?" asked the woman, turning a page.

"She volunteers here," Kate said. "We go to school together. I'm hoping that you can tell me where she lives. See, she just moved here, and I forgot her address. But I need to take something to her because she wasn't in school today."

"We don't give out volunteer addresses," the woman answered.

"This is an emergency," Kate said. "Really, I'm sure she wouldn't mind. Her name is Sasha, and—"

"Sasha?" the woman said, finally looking up. "Thin girl? Dark hair? Your age?"

Kate nodded. "That's her," she said. "I really need to find her. Do you know where she lives?"

"Sure," the woman said. "She lives here. At least she does when she gets here before six. The rest of the time, who knows?"

"No," Kate said. "My friend just volunteers here. That must be someone else. The girl I'm looking for wears a big blue gas station attendant's jacket that says 'Jack' on it."

"That's her, all right," the woman answered. "Came in here about three weeks ago."

Three weeks. That was about the same time that

Sasha had showed up at the ritual. But the woman had to be mistaken. Sasha was no runaway.

"She said she moved here from LA," Kate said.

"She told me Denver," the woman said, closing her magazine. "But a lot of them make up different stories for different people."

"Them?" Kate asked.

"The clients," the woman explained. "The runaways. They don't want us to find their real families, so they lie about where they're from."

Kate was still trying to absorb what the woman was telling her. If what she was saying was true, then Sasha lived at the Summer House. She wasn't just a volunteer. And she hadn't moved to Beecher Falls with her family. She had run away.

"Do you know if Sasha's here right now?" Kate asked. Now she wanted to talk to her more than ever. She had to find out what was going on. Part of her still insisted that this must be a big mix-up and that the woman had Sasha confused with another girl.

The woman shook her head. "She hasn't come back yet today," she said. "Sometimes she doesn't. Like I said, if the girls aren't in by six, they don't get in. But she'll turn up when she needs a bed. Do you want me to tell her you were looking for her?"

"No," Kate said. "Thanks. You've told me more than I came here looking to find out."

She left the Summer House. But she didn't know where to go. Knowing that Sasha was a runaway explained a lot of things, like why she seemed to carry everything she owned in her backpack, why she never brought a lunch to school, and why she had been so impressed by Annie's bedroom. But it brought up more questions than it answered. Kate couldn't even imagine how Sasha had managed to keep her situation hidden from them. It had to have involved a lot of planning, and being careful what she said. In some ways it was like Kate's having to hide her involvement with Wicca from everyone but Annie and Cooper. Only Sasha was hiding a much bigger secret. And now that Kate knew what it was, she had to decide what she was going to do.

Now, Kate felt even worse about having been angry at Sasha. If she really was a runaway, it explained why she was so jealous of Kate. Probably she had never had any of the things that Kate and her friends took for granted. No wonder she had wanted to be like them, no matter what it took. She had probably come to the Spring Equinox ritual hoping that she would meet people who would be nice to her.

Kate wanted to go looking for Sasha. But she had no idea where she might be or what she would say if she found her. So she just walked, thinking, until she came to a bus stop. When the bus came, she got on. As she swiped her pass through the meter, she thought again of Sasha. She didn't have a bus pass. How did she get around town? How did she get to school every day? And how was she able to go to school, anyway, if she lived in a shelter? Kate's mind was filled with questions, and no answers.

Kate signaled for the driver to stop at the next corner, where she got off. She walked up the street to Annie's house. But before she could ring the bell, the door opened and Annie stepped outside.

"Going out?" Kate asked.

"I'm going over to Cooper's," Annie said. "We were going to hang out and watch a movie or something. I think she's tired of spending most of the time over here. We looked for you after school, but you had already left. I figured you were out with Scott or something."

"I went looking for Sasha," Kate told her.

"Did you find her?" Annie asked.

"Yes and no," said Kate. "I'll tell you on the way to Cooper's."

By the time the two of them reached Cooper's street, Annie was up to speed on the Sasha situation. As Kate talked, Annie just kept shaking her head.

"A runaway?" she said over and over. "Sasha? I wonder what made her do that."

"I don't know," Kate said. "But I feel terrible about yelling at her now."

She forgot about Sasha for a moment as they stopped in front of a large house. Unlike most of the old Victorian homes in the neighborhood, the house was made of stone. Three huge slabs of granite formed steps that led up to a solid wooden door with a brass nameplate affixed to it that said THE WELTON HOUSE.

"This is where Cooper lives?" Kate said.

Annie nodded. "This is the address."

"It looks more like a museum than a house," Kate said as they ascended the steps and knocked on the door. She was sure they were in the wrong place until the door opened and Cooper's blue-haired head popped out.

"Hey, you found a Kate on your way over," Cooper said to Annie. "Cool."

Annie and Kate walked inside the house. In front of them, a wide staircase led to the second floor. The area they were standing in was filled with antiques. On the walls were portraits of serious-looking women and men in old-fashioned outfits. Everything looked freshly cleaned, and Kate noticed that there was absolutely no clutter anywhere: no mail on the hallway table, no shoes near the door, no books or magazines on any of the surfaces.

"Don't let it scare you," Cooper said, noticing that Kate and Annie were staring at the house.

"It's so beautiful," Annie said.

"It's so clean," Kate added.

Cooper snorted. "Welcome to the Welton House," she said. "Officially listed on the Washington State register of historic places, all because some guy no one has ever heard of built it."

"Welton," Annie said. "What did he do?"

"Got the Native Americans who lived here to trade him their land for some beads," Cooper said.

Kate and Annie looked at her skeptically.

"I'm serious," Cooper said. "Frederick Welton was a trader who lived here in the eighteen hundreds. He made a pile of money trapping beavers and bears and selling their skins. Somewhere along the line he made friends with the local Indian tribes. And in 1853 he convinced them to give him this land in exchange for six bear skins, seventeen beaver pelts, a rifle, and two bags of very pretty glass beads."

"You're making that up," Kate said.

"Not a word of it," Cooper informed her. "This being a historic house and all, people sometimes come through demanding tours. I've got the whole spiel down pat. But you haven't heard the best part."

"Which is?" Annie asked.

"In 1857 Frederick Welton lost all the land in an all-night poker game to a Mr. Seymour Beecher."

"As in Beecher Falls," Kate guessed.

"Exactly," said Cooper. "If it hadn't been for four queens in Beecher's hand and two pairs in Welton's, you'd be going to Welton Falls High School. All Welton had left when it was over was this house. But that still isn't the best part. That would be the ghost."

"Ghost?" Annie and Kate said in unison.

"I thought you might like that," said Cooper. "The tourists do too. See, after he lost the poker game, Welton decided he couldn't stand to lose his land. He hanged himself in his bedroom."

Kate grimaced as Cooper made a hanging gesture.

"Legend has it that Welton's ghost still walks around here," Cooper continued. "Carrying the two pairs of cards in his hand—one pair of threes and one pair of jacks. He's looking for the game that lost him everything, hoping that maybe he can talk old Beecher into another round."

"Have you ever seen him?" Kate asked.

Cooper shook her head. "Not that I remember," she said. "But my mother says that once, when I was about three, I told her that a strange man had been coming into my room at night. She searched the place, and she found a lot of old cards under the bed—only threes and jacks. She threw them all out, made me sleep in her bed for a week, and the man never came back."

"Hmmm," Annie said. "And you live here why?"

"My parents think it's very prestigious," Cooper explained. "My father is a lawyer. He likes to tell his clients that he lives in the Welton House. Even when they don't know what it is, they're impressed. And my mother brings her classes here for tours every year. She teaches third grade."

Cooper took them upstairs and showed them the rest of the house. Like the downstairs, most of the rooms were in immaculate condition, with antiques everywhere and not a spot of dust. Cooper's room, however, was a different story. Although her bed, dresser, and night stand might have been straight out of the nineteenth century, the posters on her walls were anything but. She had covered just about every square inch with pictures of her favorite singers and flyers announcing concerts by local bands.

"There's the first Limp Bizkit flyer ever," she said, pointing to a scrap of paper with ragged edges and what looked like a coffee stain on it as Annie and Kate inspected everything carefully.

"Who's this?" Kate asked, noticing a portrait hanging over Cooper's dresser. Like the ones in the hallway, it was old. The man in it had a worn-looking face with sad brown eyes. He was wearing a fur hat, and the background showed a snowy landscape.

"That's our friend Frederick himself," Cooper said. "It creeped my mother out having it downstairs, so I asked to have it in here. I thought it was fitting, since this was his bedroom anyway."

"This is where he hanged himself?" Annie asked.

"The very place," Cooper said. "From that beam up there."

Kate looked up at the thick beam that ran across

the room's ceiling. A shudder went through her as she imagined Welton hanging from it, his sad eyes staring out at nothing.

"Let's change the subject," she said.

"What? You don't like my story?" Cooper said.

"Oh, I like it," Kate said. "But I have a better one for you."

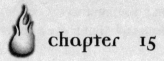 chapter 15

The rain wasn't helping things. Cooper, Annie, and Kate had been walking around the downtown area for an hour, and all they had gotten was wet. Kate's hair kept sticking to her cheeks, and she was tired of wiping it away. The rain kept running into her eyes, and inside her rubber rain jacket she was sweating like crazy, even though the temperature wasn't much above freezing.

"Remind me to tell my father not to buy these for his store again," she said, pulling futilely at the jacket. "It's like walking around in an inner tube."

Annie and Cooper weren't faring any better. Cooper's blue hair was plastered to her forehead, and Annie kept taking off her glasses, vainly trying to clean them with her fingers.

It was a gray, stormy Saturday morning. None of the stores were even open yet, and the streets were deserted. Kate had called the Summer House as soon as she thought someone might be there to answer the phone. Luckily, they had a counselor on duty in case any runaways needed help, and the woman had known who Sasha was as soon as Kate asked.

"She didn't check in last night," the woman had informed Kate. "But I wouldn't worry. She'll turn up. Sometimes she disappears for a night or two. But she comes back. Do you want me to leave a message?"

Kate hadn't left a message. She knew that would only scare Sasha away. She didn't want her to know that they knew about her situation. Not until they found her.

"I can't believe they don't turn her over to the cops," Annie said as they huddled beneath a store awning. "Isn't that what they're supposed to do with runaways?"

"They can't do anything if she won't give them a real name and address," Cooper said. "Sometimes it's better to try to help them out first, and then to find out what they're running from. Or who. My father has done some work with the charities in town, and I've heard him talking about it. Besides, some of the kids in the local music scene have spent time on the streets. It's not pretty."

"I just wish we could find her," Kate said. "She's got to be out there somewhere."

"She could be long gone," said Cooper. "If she thinks we're on to her, she might have decided to skip town. This might just be a total waste of time."

"I don't think so," Kate replied. "Something

tells me that we're going to find her if we just keep looking."

The rain let up a little, and they started walking again. Some of the stores were opening and people were beginning to appear, running into coffee shops for muffins and something to drink, or picking up newspapers. Kate looked at their faces, hoping one of them would turn out to be Sasha.

They searched for another hour, looking everywhere they thought a girl trying to keep out of the rain might be, but there was no sign of Sasha anywhere. Cooper was right—they couldn't look everywhere, and Sasha could be in any of a thousand places. Finally, Kate admitted defeat, and the three of them went to the bus stop to wait for a ride home.

When the bus pulled up, Kate stepped aside to let the passengers off. She was surprised to see that Sherrie was the first person to emerge. Jessica and Tara were right behind her, and following up the rear was Sasha.

"Well, what have we here?" Sherrie purred when she saw Kate, Cooper, and Annie standing there soaked to the skin. "You three look like you've been having a morning swim." She opened an umbrella she was carrying and stood beneath it while Tara, Sasha, and Jessica tried to cram in around her to keep dry.

"What are you guys doing out?" Kate asked. She wanted to drag Sasha away and talk to her, but she knew she couldn't do that or Sherrie would want to know what was going on.

"We had a sleepover at Jess's last night," Tara said. "We tried to invite you, but your mother said you were doing something else."

"And now we're going to do a little shopping," Sherrie said. "We'd ask you to come, but I don't think you'd want to drip all over the store."

The whole time they were talking, Kate was trying to steal glances at Sasha. She needed to figure out a way to talk to her without Sherrie and the others interfering. But how could she do it?

"You know," Annie said suddenly, "Sasha could really use a makeover. It might be fun to go buy some new clothes and some makeup. You know, glam her up a little."

Sherrie turned her head and looked at Sasha. "Crandall might be right," she said. "I bet there's a real knockout underneath that flannel. What do you say, Sash? Are you up for it?"

"I mean really, how much can it cost?" Annie said. "Thirty, forty bucks?"

"Where do you shop?" Sherrie said dismissively. "If we're doing this, we're going to do it right."

Sasha was looking very uncomfortable. At first, Kate had no idea what Annie was doing. Why would she suggest a makeover? Then, as she watched Sasha waver, she got it. Annie knew that Sasha didn't have any money. And if she thought that hanging out with Sherrie and the gang meant that she had to spend some, she would find a way out.

"Oh, it would be great!" Tara said to Sasha. "I know this place that has the best shoes."

"And we could get your hair done," Jessica suggested. "I think the place I go is having a special—thirty-five dollars for the whole works."

"I don't know," Sasha said.

"If it's about the money . . ." Sherrie said, inadvertently falling right into Annie's trap.

"Oh, no," Sasha said. "It's not that. It's just that I promised my mother I would help her look at houses today. She thinks she found one that she likes. In fact, I should probably go meet her. Why don't you guys go on, and we'll do this another day."

"It's not every day we offer to turn someone into a princess," Sherrie said. "But fine, we can do it next weekend."

"Sure," Sasha said. "You're on."

"Well, we should get going, girls," Sherrie said to Jessica and Tara. "If we stand here much longer, we'll end up looking like these three."

The three of them ran off, still huddled under Sherrie's umbrella. As soon as they were gone, Kate turned to Sasha.

"We need to talk," she said.

"What about?" asked Sasha. "I thought you wanted me to stay out of your way."

Kate looked down, noticing for the first time how old and ragged Sasha's sneakers were.

"I'm sorry about that," Kate said. "Scott told me what you said to him at the Frozen Cow."

"He did?" Sasha said, as if she couldn't believe it. "So you know that I wasn't trying to get him to go out with me?"

Kate nodded. She didn't know how to say what she needed to say next. "Want to get some breakfast?" she asked.

"Well, I'm supposed to meet my mother," Sasha said. "The house and all."

"It's on me," Kate said.

"I guess I can be a *little* late," Sasha answered.

The four of them ran through the rain to a coffee shop. They went to a booth in the back and sat down. Little rivers of water ran from their clothes onto the floor, but Kate didn't even notice. She was too busy trying to think of how to best handle the situation.

"Thanks for saving me from the makeover," Sasha said to Annie as they looked over the menus.

"I had an idea that wasn't exactly your thing," Annie said kindly.

"I like those girls," Sasha said. "But sometimes it's hard to keep up."

"Tell me about it," Kate said, closing her menu as the waitress came over and took their orders.

While they waited for their food to arrive, they talked about things like music and movies. Sasha was very animated, telling stories about her life in Los Angeles. As Kate listened, she wondered how much of what Sasha said—if anything—was true and what was made up.

When the food came, Sasha dove into her stack of pancakes while the others ate more slowly. She had finished nearly all of her breakfast while they were still working on the first halves of theirs.

"Do you want my bacon?" Cooper asked her. "I don't eat meat."

After Sasha had slowed down a little bit, Kate decided to test the waters. "Sasha, I want you to know that I didn't say anything to Rowan or the others," she said.

Sasha nodded, chewing on her bacon. "I know," she said. "I talked to them later on. They said that they just don't think I'm ready yet. Whatever. I don't really care. I was in a coven back in LA, so I don't need any year of dedication. I was just doing it because you guys seemed into it."

"I just wanted you to know that I didn't have anything to do with that," Kate repeated.

"Man, I wish my mom made breakfasts like this," Sasha said, taking another bite of pancakes. "It's usually just cold cereal."

"Sasha, we know where you live," Kate said gently.

Sasha stopped eating and looked at her. "You mean with my parents' friends?" she said hesitantly.

"No," Kate said. "At the Summer House."

Sasha laughed. "I don't live there," she said. "I told you—I volunteer there."

"I went there," Kate said. "I was looking for you to tell you that I was sorry about the misunderstanding over Scott. I thought they might have your address. The woman there told me that you stay there."

"Patrice?" Sasha said. "She was just fooling with you. She does that all the time. I don't live at that dump. My parents are about to move into a big, new house."

Kate looked at Annie and Cooper for help. She didn't know what to say to Sasha.

"Sasha, it's okay if you're not what you told us you are," Annie said. "If you're—" She stopped as Sasha glared at her.

"If I'm what?" she said angrily. "Look, I don't know what you guys think, but you're wrong. I thought you were supposed to be my friends."

"We are," Cooper said. "That's why we're trying to talk to you."

"I don't hear any talking," Sasha said, putting her fork down. "I just hear you accusing me of being a liar. Just like Kate did before. Well, she was wrong about that, and she's wrong about this. She just heard wrong. I don't live at the Summer House."

"They told me that you've been there for three weeks," Kate said. "And that you told them you're from Denver, not LA."

"What did you do?" Sasha asked. "Run a police report on me or something? Who are you going to believe, some woman you've never met or me?"

"It's okay," Kate said, trying to soothe Sasha, who was becoming more and more agitated. "We just want to help you."

"I don't need any help!" Sasha said. "And I definitely don't need you three nosing around in my business."

She stood up, knocking over a glass of milk. As Kate scrambled to find some napkins and wipe up the flowing liquid, Sasha grabbed her backpack.

"You were right, Kate," she said. "I should have stayed out of your way."

"Sasha," Kate begged. "Sit down. We just want to talk."

But Sasha was already headed for the door.

chapter 16

"You did the right thing," Sophia said as Kate sat across from her in the back room of Crones' Circle.

Kate held a steaming mug of tea in her hands. Cooper and Annie, seated on the couch, were also drinking tea. Their wet coats and shoes were scattered over the floor and the backs of chairs, drying.

They'd gone there after Sasha ran out of the coffee shop. Kate didn't know who else to turn to. She felt as if she'd made the biggest mistake yet.

"But what if something happens to her?" she asked Sophia. "It will be all my fault. I should have just kept my mouth shut."

"No," said Sophia. "You needed to tell her that you know about her situation. It would have come out sometime anyway. She couldn't maintain a lie that big for much longer."

"What do you think she'll do now?" Annie asked.

Sophia shook her head. "That I can't say. I don't think she'll go very far, especially if she doesn't have any money."

Archer came into the room from the store's office. "I just talked to a friend of mine who works at the Summer House," she said. "He promised to call us if Sasha goes back there. I also called Thea."

"Who's Thea?" Kate asked.

"She's a member of our coven," Sophia explained. "She works with the children's services department of the city."

"Not the police!" Kate exclaimed.

"No," said Sophia. "Not the police. Thea helps kids who are in trouble—runaways, homeless kids, kids in bad situations. If we find Sasha, Thea may be able to help her."

"What can she do?" Cooper asked.

"That depends on the situation," Sophia answered. "If her parents are looking for her, they'll have to be notified. We'll also have to find out where she's from and why she ran away. Thea will know everything that has to be done."

"I guess this is what Rowan meant by being part of a community," Annie said.

"We like to call it the Broomstick Mafia," Archer said, making them all laugh and breaking some of the tension.

"Shouldn't we be out there looking for her?" Kate said. "I feel so helpless just sitting here like this."

"The best thing you can do is go home and get some rest," Sophia told her. "You've put the word out. Now wait and see what happens. It's like magic—sometimes it just takes a little time."

After drying out a little more, Kate, Annie, and Cooper did go home. It was still raining, and Kate hoped that Sasha was at least somewhere warm and dry. She still couldn't help but think that if it weren't for her Sasha would at least be safely inside. Instead, she was running around in the cold and the wet with no place to go and no one to help her.

The girls split up at the bus stop, each of them going to her own house to change and wait for news from Sophia. Kate tried to distract herself by working on some homework, but she couldn't concentrate. She just kept seeing Sasha's frightened face. Finally she gave up and sat, looking out the window, for the rest of the day. She was so quiet at dinner that when her mother asked her if anything was wrong, Kate wanted to break down and tell her everything, but she knew she couldn't. Her parents just wouldn't understand about the whole Wicca connection, and she couldn't really tell them about Sasha without getting into that too. So she just said she wasn't feeling very well and asked to be excused. When the phone rang later on, she grabbed it quickly, hoping it would be Sophia or Archer.

"Hey there," said Scott. "How's my favorite girl?"

Kate almost started to cry, but she was able to stop herself. Again she wanted to tell Scott everything about Sasha's disappearance. But she didn't want anyone else from school to know, in case Sasha hadn't really run off and was just hiding out. So she pushed Sasha as far as she could into the back of her mind and tried to sound as if everything was fine instead of being the mess that it was.

She talked to Scott for a while, barely paying attention to the conversation, then hung up. She looked at the clock. It was almost ten o'clock. If Sasha hadn't turned up by now, she probably wasn't going to. Kate got into bed, keeping the phone nearby just in case, and turned out the light.

She tossed and turned for a while, listening to the rain outside and trying to get the image of Sasha huddled in a dirty alley or walking alone on the streets out of her mind. Finally, when she was totally exhausted, she fell into a restless sleep.

She woke up the next morning feeling worse than she had the night before. It was still raining, and everything outside her window was gray and depressing. She didn't even feel like getting out of bed. She just wanted to stay there, wrapped in the warm blankets, pretending that it had all been a bad dream. But before she could even close her eyes and try to get back to sleep there was a knock on her door and her mother peered in.

"Time to get up," she said. "Breakfast is almost done, and then we're going to mass."

Kate smiled weakly. "I'll be right down," she said.

Church that morning seemed to last forever. Kate was distracted, and found herself looking at the stained glass windows. Her favorite was of Mary, whose face had a kind expression, and she looked out at Kate with eyes that were full of joy and happiness. *Just like the eyes of Gaia*, Kate thought as she stared at the window. The expression on Mary's face reminded Kate very much of the image of the goddess she had seen in her meditation at the Spring Equinox ritual and it sparked an idea.

When she got home from church, she went up to her bedroom and took out a small white votive candle. Lighting it, she said "Gaia. I need your help. Please help me find Sasha. Please keep her safe. Please help her understand that I just want to be her friend." She sat back, and something about the small ritual she'd just done seemed right. She watched the candle burn for a minute, then blew it out to answer the phone.

"Kate, it's Cooper. I'm at Crones' Circle. Sasha's here."

Kate hung up. Not even stopping to change out of her church clothes, she ran out the door, telling her startled parents that she would be back in a little while. At the bus stop she paced nervously, willing a bus to come soon. Finally one appeared, and she got on.

When she reached her stop, she practically flew to the door of Crones' Circle, arriving tired and panting. Inside, she found Annie and Cooper in the back room, along with Sophia, Archer, and a woman she remembered seeing at the Equinox ritual; she guessed this was Thea. And in the center of the room, seated in an armchair and wrapped in a big, warm blanket, was Sasha.

Kate wanted to run to Sasha and hug her, but she didn't know if she should. Instead, she just stood in front of her, not knowing what to say.

"Hi," she said finally, feeling like a total idiot.

"Hi," Sasha said back, sounding tired.

"I'm sorry about yesterday," said Kate.

Sasha sighed. "It's okay," she said. "I should have known someone would figure it out sooner or later. When you told me that you knew, I just panicked. I was afraid someone would try to make me go back. I wandered around for a long time, trying to think of somewhere to go. But there wasn't anywhere. I was afraid to go back to the Summer House. So I sat under the steps at the beach, watching the ocean all night. And this morning I decided to come here. I don't know why. I just happened to think of it, and when I got here they were just opening."

"Sasha's been telling us some of her story," Thea told Kate. "She was in a foster home, and she had some problems there. That's why she ran away."

"So you're not really from LA?" Kate asked.

Sasha shook her head. "I've never even been to LA," she said. "I just made up details about it from things I've seen on TV. There's no Jack, either, in case you were going to ask. I found the jacket in a thrift store."

"He didn't sound like a very good catch anyway," Kate said.

Sasha smiled. Then she started to cry. This time, Kate did go and hug her. Sasha hugged her back, her chest heaving as she sobbed, her hands holding tightly to Kate's body. When she finally stopped, and Kate pulled away, her face was red with tears.

"What's going to happen to me?" she asked.

Kate looked at Thea.

"I'll have to make a few calls tomorrow morning," Thea said. "But because I work for children's services, I should be able to keep Sasha under my supervision. She can come stay with me until we figure out what to do next."

"It's going to be okay," Kate said to Sasha. "See?"

"I don't know what I would have done without all of you," Sasha said.

"Well, you certainly have made life more exciting around here," Cooper commented. "I'll give you that."

"Take that as a compliment," Annie told Sasha.

"That's about as good as it gets, coming from her."

Kate left the others talking to Sasha and went into the store's little kitchen, where Sophia was making more tea.

"Will she really be all right?" Kate asked.

Sophia stirred sugar into a mug. "We'll have to wait and see," she said. "Thea has a lot of experience with troubled teenagers. We'll have to find out why Sasha had problems in foster care and what other issues she has."

"What about her parents?" Kate asked. "Will you have to contact them?"

"She says her parents aren't in the picture," Sophia answered. "She didn't say whether that means they're dead or just neglectful. But if she was in foster care at her age, there's a good chance she's been given up."

"That's so sad," Kate said. "I'm glad she found the flyer about the ritual. Otherwise we never would have been able to help her."

Sophia took a sip of tea. "There's not a lot I'm sure about in this life," she said. "But one thing I know—nothing is just an accident. There was a reason Sasha found that flyer, just like there was a reason you found that spell book. You don't always know what the reason is right away. Sometimes you don't know for many years. But eventually, you find out."

They went back and joined the others, talking for a while until Archer noticed that Sasha had fallen asleep in her chair.

"Looks like someone needs to get to a nice, warm bed," Thea said. "I'll take her home now."

"Can we call her later?" Kate asked, getting up to go.

"How about tomorrow night?" Thea suggested, writing her number down on a piece of paper and handing it to Kate.

Kate left with Cooper and Annie. When they stepped outside, Kate noticed that it had finally stopped raining. As they walked to the bus stop, she thought about how thankful she was that Sasha had come back and was safe. Then she thought about the ritual she'd done earlier. Had the two been connected?

"What time does Crones' Circle open on Sundays?" she asked.

"Eleven," Annie answered. "Why?"

Kate did the math in her head. Sasha had decided to go to the store right before it opened. Kate had lit her candle and said her prayer at around ten-thirty. "No reason," she said to Annie. "I was just curious."

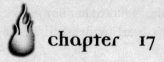

chapter 17

Kate wondered how long she had been standing in the darkness, waiting. She had lost all track of time, but it seemed like forever. The blindfold over her eyes kept out all light, not that it would have mattered. They had turned out the lights anyway. The only connection she had to the world was the random rustling sounds of the others as they also waited and the sound of the drum beating softly in the other room.

She was in the storage room of Crones' Circle, along with the other people who had decided to take part in the dedication ritual. But she had no idea what was going to happen. Archer had put the blindfold on her and told her to wait.

She decided to go over her dedication statement once more. They had each been told to prepare something short to say during the ritual—something that said what they were promising to do and what they hoped to gain. Kate had spent most of Monday night writing hers. She'd read it about a hundred times, but she was still afraid she would forget something when the time came. She focused, saying the words in her head as she waited.

Then she sensed movement as somebody came into the room and passed by her without saying anything. She felt a body momentarily pressed against hers, and then it was gone, as if someone had left the room.

Twice more she sensed someone coming into the storage area and then leaving again. What was going on? Why was she still standing there? For a moment she had the horrible thought that they were playing a joke on her, and she almost tore the blindfold off to see what was happening. But she calmed herself by listening to the beating of the drum and reminding herself that no one from the Coven of the Green Wood or the store would let anything bad happen to her.

Then someone took her hand, startling her. But the person's touch was gentle and reassuring, and she instantly calmed down. She felt herself being urged forward, and she took a hesitant step. Another hand on her elbow steadied her even more, and she let herself be led forward into the other room.

She was still disoriented, and had no idea where in the room she was. The hands guiding her moved her forward and then stopped. When they let go of her, she was again alone, standing in the dark. But this time she was excited. The drumming was all around her now, and she could feel a faint heat on her skin.

Several more minutes went by during which the only sound came from the drum. The rhythm of it was hypnotic, and Kate found herself wanting to dance. But she remained still, waiting, and after a while the drumming stopped. Now there was total silence.

"Welcome," said a voice that Kate recognized as Rowan's. "And blessed be."

"Blessed be," said a chorus of voices all around Kate, giving the traditional witches' greeting.

"Tonight you come to the circle to begin a journey," Rowan continued. "A journey that will last for a year and a day and will take you into a world with many surprises and many challenges. You have come here to take your first step on that journey, to dedicate yourselves to walking the path. While others are with you, you will take this journey alone. So if any of you are not ready to begin the journey, you may turn back now."

Rowan paused, waiting. Kate let Rowan's words fill her mind. They made her feel excited—excited and a little scared. She really *was* setting out on an adventure. Deciding to commit herself to learning as much as she could about Wicca was an important step in her life. It wasn't just deciding to read a book or try out a meditation. It meant she could help people—people like Sasha. It was something that could change her life forever. She'd thought long and hard about it, and although she still had some fears, she was sure that it was the right thing to do.

"If you are ready," Rowan said, "it is time to take your first step. Remove your blindfolds."

Kate reached behind her and fumbled with the knot holding the blindfold closed. She worked it free and pulled the cloth from around her head.

The room was filled with what looked like hundreds of white candles. Everywhere Kate looked tiny flames lit up the walls and the faces of the people standing in a circle around the room. The light transformed the room into a magical grove, and the circle of people dressed in white robes made Kate feel as if she'd stepped out of time. Kate and the others were all standing at one side of the circle. On the other side sat a large cauldron. Flames leapt up from inside it, but there was no smoke. Behind the cauldron stood Rowan, with Anya on one side of her and Sophia on the other.

Annie and Cooper were on either side of Kate. It felt good to have her two best friends with her, and Kate was glad that all three of them had decided to participate in the ritual. Although she knew that what Rowan had said was right, and that she'd be taking her journey on her own, she would also have Cooper and Annie beside her to help her if she needed them.

"Merry meet," Anya said, stepping forward. "You have taken the first step onto the path. It will be the first of many. For the next year and a day, through one full turn of the Wheel of the Year, you will be travelers in the realm of the Lady and the Lord. They will greet you in many forms. They will answer your questions, and they will ask questions of you. Tonight you come before us, your community, to tell us what gifts you bring on this journey and what you hope to find at its end. Each of you will be called to speak. You will then be given a light to help you see your way on the path, as well as a word of power. This word represents one of your challenges for the year. Now, who will be the first to come to the cauldron?"

Annie stepped forward immediately. Kate watched as her friend walked across the room and stood in front of the burning cauldron and the women behind it.

"Merry meet," Rowan said to Annie.

"Merry meet," Annie replied, her voice softer than usual.

"Are you prepared to begin your journey?" Rowan asked, and Annie nodded.

"What gifts do you bring with you?" Anya asked her.

"I bring with me the gifts of curiosity, honesty, and patience," Annie said.

"These are good gifts," Sophia said. She was carrying in her hands a bowl, which she held out to Annie. "Take a word from the bowl and read it."

Annie reached inside and pulled out a slip of paper. Unfolding it, she read, "Healing."

Sophia smiled. "That is your challenge," she said. "Use your gifts to meet it."

Rowan took a candle and, dipping a match into the cauldron's flames, lit it. As she handed the candle to Annie she said, "This candle burns with the light of inspiration. May it light your way as you travel. Now go and become part of the circle."

Annie stepped away from the cauldron, taking a place in the ring of people surrounding the remaining dedicants. Kate waited as Anya called for the next person to step forward. For some reason, Kate couldn't get herself to move. She wanted to, but it was as if her body was frozen. She watched as one of the men took his place before the cauldron and answered the questions put to him.

Two more people went forward. Then, at Anya's call, Cooper moved away from Kate and stood before the flames.

"What gifts do you bring with you?" Anya asked.

Cooper cleared her throat. "I bring on my journey the gifts of loyalty, creativity, and perseverance," she said in a firm voice.

Sophia held out the bowl and instructed Cooper to take a word. She picked one quickly and read it. "Connection," she read, sounding slightly perplexed before moving on to take her candle and a place in the circle.

Kate thought about the gifts Cooper and Annie had listed. They hadn't discussed what they were going to say, and it was interesting to see what each of them had chosen. Annie, the scientist, *was* curious. *And she's definitely honest*, Kate thought to herself. And as for patience, she had shown a lot of that in helping Kate through her early disasters with magic.

Cooper too, was all the things she said she was. No one would deny that she was a loyal friend. *More loyal than I was*, Kate thought sadly as she remembered how she had once pretended not to be friends with Annie and Cooper. And Cooper's music was only one of the ways in which she was creative. As for perseverance, well, Kate didn't think there was anyone who would argue with that assessment.

But what about her own gifts? She had thought hard about what she was going to say when her turn came. A lot of things had gone through her mind, but none of them had seemed perfect. Was that why she was hesitating about going forward? Was she afraid that her gifts weren't good enough? But what if they were all she had to give? Did that mean she shouldn't attempt the task she'd set for herself? Should she just admit that she had made a mistake, and that she wasn't ready to seriously study witchcraft?

A young woman was standing in front of Anya and the others, answering their questions. Kate realized that she was the only one left standing in the circle. Everyone else had stepped forward. When the girl was done, there would be no one else to go instead of Kate. Her heart beat faster as she listened to the young woman finish her statements and take her word from Sophia's bowl.

"Who will come to the cauldron?" Anya called for the last time.

Kate couldn't move. She was scared. What if she was making the wrong decision? What if she really wasn't cut out for this? She'd thought she was sure, but now her mind was flooded with questions. Then she looked over and saw Annie and Cooper standing with the others who had taken part in the ritual. Their candles glowed brightly, and they were smiling at her.

She stepped forward. Once she made that first tentative step, it was easy. She walked up to the cauldron and faced Anya.

"What gifts do you bring with you on your journey?" she asked.

Kate lifted her head and looked into Anya's eyes.

"I bring with me the gifts of willingness, friendship, and doubt," she said.

Anya's eyes sparkled as she stepped aside, and Sophia moved in front of Kate.

"These are *very* good gifts, indeed," she said, giving Kate a private smile. "Now, choose your challenge."

Kate took a deep breath and reached into the bowl. Her fingers moved among the many different pieces of paper until she selected one and took it out.

"Truth," she read.

As Sophia handed her a candle and she went to stand beside her friends, Kate thought about what her challenge might mean. Did it mean that she had to start telling the truth? She pretty much already did that, at least most of the time. Maybe it meant that she had to find out the truth about something else. But what? She had no idea. Was it possible that she'd chosen the wrong word? She didn't know. *I suppose I'll find out*, she thought to herself.

"Your journey is now begun," Rowan said. "As you travel, remember your gifts. Remember also your challenges. They will appear to you in many forms, some recognizable and some not. But however they come, your gifts will help you to face them."

"And as you travel," Sophia said. "Remember that there are others traveling the same path. Some of them are with you here tonight. Others you have yet to meet."

"But when you do," Rowan said, concluding the ritual, "remember the words with which we open all our circles."

Kate joined the others in saying the phrase that was quickly becoming familiar to her: "Merry meet, and merry part, and merry meet again!"

With the ritual over, the lights were turned back on and the participants talked freely with one another as they helped blow out the candles and put the furniture in the room back into place.

"That felt so great," Cooper said as she, Kate, and Annie carried a table into the center of the room.

"I'm a little confused about my challenge, though," Annie said. "Healing? What's that supposed to mean?"

"Try getting connection," Cooper said. "It sounds like I'm going to be set up on a blind date or something."

Kate was glad to hear that her friends were as perplexed about their challenges as she was about hers. At least that way she wouldn't be the only one with no clue about what she was supposed to be looking for while she studied Wicca.

"You guys were *so* cool!" said a voice behind Kate.

She turned and saw Sasha standing there. She was wearing new clothes, and she looked better than Kate had ever seen her.

"Hey," Kate said, hugging her. "How is everything?"

"Pretty good," Sasha answered. "Thea has been great. She's helping me sort everything out. I'm still not sure exactly what I want to do, but she says I can stay with her as long as I need to."

"That's fantastic," Cooper said, giving Sasha a high-five.

"I really want to thank you guys again," Sasha said. "Especially you, Kate. You could have just given up on me, but you didn't."

Kate shrugged. "And let you run off to tour around with Jack and No Doubt?" she said. "I don't think so."

Archer had pulled back the curtains that separated the ritual room from the rest of the store. People were leaving, and Kate noticed that Tyler was standing by the door talking to someone.

"I'll be right back," she said to her friends. "There's something I have to do."

As she walked toward Tyler, she bumped into someone who was crouched down, perusing some books on a lower shelf.

"Oh, excuse me," Kate said, realizing suddenly she was looking down at the back of one of the girls from the school cheerleading squad. Before Megan could turn around, Kate spun around in alarm and continued toward Tyler. *She didn't see me*, Kate told herself. *She couldn't have.*

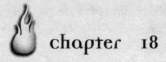

chapter 18

It was *not* a date.

Kate sat at a booth in the back of the burger place on the pier, waiting for Tyler to arrive. She'd decided that she needed to explain things to him. It was time for her to tell him about Scott and about why she had acted so strangely on the night they'd gone out. She hoped he would understand. She really did like him, and she wanted to be friends, especially if she was going to run into him at rituals or at the bookstore.

She hadn't told Scott that she was going to meet Tyler. Luckily, she hadn't had to make up any excuse, either. Scott was out with his friends. He assumed that Kate was home doing home-work, and she didn't see any reason to tell him otherwise.

While she waited, Kate played with the new ring on her finger. It had been a gift from Scott, to replace the one she'd thrown into the ocean when he broke up with her. But there was no chance of this one getting thrown away. She'd learned her lesson. Scott was definitely the guy for her, and now that things were all set with his school, she was perfectly content.

"You got the same booth," Tyler said, sliding into the seat across from Kate.

"It wasn't on purpose," she said. "I just asked for one in the back."

Now that Tyler was there, Kate decided to just say what she had to say. "I'm glad you came," she said. "I thought maybe you'd be mad."

"Not mad," Tyler said. "A little confused, maybe, but not mad."

"I don't blame you for that," Kate said. "You deserve an explanation."

"It's okay," said Tyler. "You don't have to explain. I'm just not your type, right?"

"No," said Kate. "I mean, no, that's not it. It's just that I have a boyfriend."

Tyler nodded. "Boyfriend," he repeated.

Kate played with the salt and pepper shakers. "Yeah," she said. "His name is Scott. He's a football player." She didn't know why she was telling Tyler all of this, but she was nervous, and when she was nervous she talked too much.

"Football player," Tyler said. "Should I watch my back?"

Kate laughed in spite of herself. "Don't

worry," she said. "He doesn't know. And anyway, we were broken up when you and I had our . . . when we had dinner. But we got back together."

"Well, that explains everything, then," Tyler said. "Shall we order?"

Kate looked up at him. "You still want to be friends with me?" she asked. "After what I did?"

"You didn't *do* anything," said Tyler. "Remember?"

Kate blushed. "You know what I mean."

"Look," Tyler said. "I think you're great. That doesn't mean I have to date you. If all we can be is friends, then that's fine."

"Are you sure you're a guy?" Kate asked.

Tyler laughed. "Try growing up with a mom and a sister telling you how you have to be sensitive your whole life," he said. "It rubs off after a while."

They ordered their food and continued talking while they ate. Kate was so relieved that Tyler wasn't angry with her that she was much more comfortable being around him than she'd been the first time they'd had dinner. She even found herself stealing fries off his plate when she finished hers.

"Hey," he said. "You owe me for those."

"How about I buy you an ice cream after dinner?" Kate suggested.

"You're on," Tyler agreed.

When they finished, they walked over to the Frozen Cow, and Kate made good on her promise by getting Tyler a butter pecan cone and a strawberry one for herself. Because the ice cream parlor was crowded, they decided to walk along the beach.

"Ice cream in April," Kate said as they walked. "Maybe not the best idea."

"Yeah, but just think how cool it still is," Tyler said, giving his cone a lick. "At least the ice cream won't drip."

They walked until they came to the giant boulder. Climbing the rocks leading to the top, they sat down to finish their ice cream. The night was clear, and the sky stretched out above them filled with stars.

"I liked what you said at the dedication ritual," Tyler said to Kate. "About doubt being one of your gifts."

"I don't really know why I said that," Kate admitted. "I'd actually planned on saying positivity, but someone else did. I thought it would look like I was copying if I said it too. Doubt just kind of popped out at the last second."

"And do you have doubts?" Tyler asked. "About Wicca, I mean."

"Some," Kate said. "But that's why I decided to do this year-and-a-day thing. I want to find out what it's all about and whether or not it's for me.

I don't know that I can believe all the things your mother does, for example. Or that you do. But I want to find out."

"That's one of the great things about witch-craft," Tyler said. "You don't have to believe any one set of things. You'll discover pretty quickly that people believe all kinds of things. People who say that their way is the only right way are probably afraid that their way really *isn't* the right one."

"Do you ever have doubts?" Kate asked.

"Sure," Tyler said. "All the time."

"And how do you deal with them?"

Tyler crunched his cone. "You just have to take risks sometimes," he said. "Sometimes things seem really safe, you know? You think you've made the right choice or you know exactly what you want. Then something happens and you're not sure. It's easy to run back to that original thing instead of taking a chance. But sometimes you need to take a chance too."

"Like Sasha running away instead of taking a chance on us helping her," Kate said.

"Right," said Tyler. "But she did take a chance, and now she has a lot of people who care about her."

They sat in silence for a while, looking at the stars and the ocean. *Do I take enough chances?* Kate wondered. She'd definitely taken a chance when she approached Annie about checking out the spell book in the school library. But she'd only done it when she had no other choice. What about other times? Did she usually stick with what was familiar, or did she let herself try new things?

She thought about her life. Sherrie, Jessica, and Tara were familiar. And she was having a hard time letting go of them, even though part of her thought she would be better off without them. She also was having a hard time letting go of some of her beliefs about religion and what it should be. But she was doing it, slowly, and it felt good, even when it was hard. So maybe she was making progress after all.

But what about Scott? a voice in her head asked.

What about Scott? Scott was the one thing she was sure of. Or was she? She asked herself why she was really with him. Was it because he made her happy? Or was it because he was safe? Did being with him make her feel secure because it meant she didn't have to take any risks?

She looked over at Tyler. She remembered the first time she'd seen him, and how she'd been drawn in by his golden eyes. It was true—he was really cute. But there was more to him than that. A lot more. She'd never talked with a guy the way she talked with Tyler. He made her ask questions. He made her look at things in a different way. He made her look for the truth.

The truth. Wasn't that what her challenge was—the truth? She hadn't really understood what that meant. But maybe this was part of it. Maybe she was being asked to look at herself and find out what the true parts were and what parts were holding her back.

But was being with Scott holding her back? She felt the ring on her finger. She'd been so happy when Scott said he wanted to get back together. She was sure they were meant to be together. But was it because she missed having him in her life, or because having him back made things feel more normal? And where did Tyler fit into all of this?

"Tyler?" she said suddenly.

"Yeah?" he responded, wiping ice cream from his chin.

"There's something I didn't tell you the night we went out," she said, feeling her pulse begin to speed up as she made a decision.

"What's that?" asked Tyler.

"This," said Kate. She leaned over and kissed him, catching him off guard. Her lips pressed against his, and she put her hands around his neck.

She knew what she was doing was crazy. She'd just finished telling him that she had a boyfriend, and here she was kissing him. What was he going to think?

She didn't care. It felt so good to have her mouth on his, and to feel him in her arms. When he slid his hands around her and pulled her closer, she knew she'd done the right thing. He held her tightly, kissing her lips, then her chin and her cheeks.

She didn't know what she was going to do about Scott. All she knew at that moment was that she felt as if she and Tyler were the only two people in the world. Nothing else mattered. She had taken a chance, allowed herself to risk making a mistake. And it felt wonderful.

When Tyler finally pulled away from her, she found herself staring into his eyes, unable to say anything. She was afraid that anything that came out of her mouth would ruin what had just happened.

"Was this a good thing?" Tyler said.

"Yeah," Kate said. "It was a good thing."

"Okay," Tyler said, grinning. "Because I'd really like to do it again."

When she got home, Kate went to her room and flopped onto her bed. She and Tyler had spent a long time on top of the rock at the edge of the ocean, talking and kissing. *But mostly kissing*, she said to herself, trying to remember exactly how Tyler tasted, smelled, and felt.

She put her hands to her face, breathing in the

scent of him. The ring on her finger scratched her nose, and she thought suddenly of Scott. She would have to talk to him, and soon. There could be no putting it off. She knew that being with him wasn't what she really wanted, even if it was the easiest thing to do. But what was he going to say? He had changed his college plans just to be near her. He had given up a scholarship to the school in New York. And now she was going to have to tell him that she didn't want to be with him. Thinking about it, the joy inside her turned to icy fear. Breaking up with Scott—again—was going to change a lot of things in her life.

But she knew she had to. And she knew that she could do it. She'd learned a lot about herself in the last few weeks. She'd been able to put aside her fears and help Sasha. She'd taken part in the dedication ritual and accepted the challenge of going deeper into Wicca. This was just one more challenge.

Better sooner than later, she told herself. She might as well call Scott and talk to him that night. If she waited, she would only worry about it. She started to pick up the phone to dial his number, but it rang before she could.

"Hello?" she said.

"Oh, you're home." It was Sherrie.

"Hey," Kate said. "Can I call you right back?" She wanted to get the conversation with Scott over with before she did anything else.

"Oh, this will take just a second," Sherrie responded.

"Okay," said Kate. "What's up?"

"I'm just sitting here with the girls," Sherrie said. "And we were thinking about you."

"Really?" said Kate. "Why?" It wasn't like Sherrie to just call for no reason. Something had to be going on.

"I had an interesting talk with Megan at practice today," Sherrie replied.

Megan. The icy feeling in Kate's stomach got worse.

"She said she saw you at that witch store in town the other night," Sherrie continued. "You and your friends. She said you seemed awfully friendly with the people there."

So, Megan *had* seen them at Crones' Circle the night of the ceremony.

"I can imagine Crandall and Rivers hanging out with freaks like that," Sherrie said when Kate didn't respond. "But you? What's with that? Are you becoming a witch or something?"

Kate started to tell Sherrie that she was being ridiculous and that Megan had blown things all out of proportion. But then she stopped herself. Her challenge was truth. She'd already told the truth once by admitting that she wanted to be with Tyler. Now she had another chance. But telling Sherrie that she was studying Wicca would be like publishing a notice in the newspaper. Could she really do it?

Kate took a deep breath. Sherrie was waiting for an answer.

She couldn't breathe.

Something was in her mouth. A rag. It tasted of dirt and oil and something else she couldn't place, like overly sweet cough syrup. Her head hurt, and a lingering chemical scent filled her nose as she tried to pull air into her lungs. She attempted to spit out the rag, but it was held there with something that wound tightly around her head. When she tried to bring her hands to her face, she found that they too, were bound.

Tape, she thought, a dim recognition flashing briefly through the haze that engulfed her mind. *It's tape.*

She tried to clear her head, to make the memories come, but the harder she tried the more confused she became. Where was she? Why was there a rag in her mouth? Why were her hands tied? She realized suddenly that she was lying on her side and that she was in a very small space. But it was dark, and she couldn't see anything. Why? Was there something over her eyes, or were they just closed?

She tried blinking, and found that her eyelids didn't want to do what she asked of them. It was as if they were weighted down, shut tightly despite her fierce desire to will them open.

Finally she managed to open them a tiny bit, and even that was an enormous effort. But still she saw nothing. She was in total darkness. No light shone; there was just a fuzzy gray distortion in the blackness. Exhausted from the effort of trying to see, she let her eyes close again, almost thankfully, and concentrated on breathing. Her chest ached, and each small stream of stale air that moved through her nose brought new pain.

She knew she had to get free. But she couldn't move. Every new effort was met with resistance from the tape that circled her wrists, and she found that her ankles were also bound. She couldn't cry out for help because of the rag. And then the chemical smell came again, and she felt her thoughts becoming muddied, like the moon disappearing behind clouds. She tried one final time to breathe, and it was like hands closing around her throat.

Cooper Rivers sat up in bed, gasping. She reached for her mouth, realized that nothing was filling it and that her hands were free, and looked frantically around her. It was still night. She was in darkness, but the window across from her bed was filled with moonlight, which illuminated the familiar dresser, chair, and other contents of her room. Almost reluctantly, she let herself fall back against her pillows.

The dream had seemed so real. Even now she rubbed her wrists and moved her feet against one another beneath the sheets, making sure they were indeed free. She could feel, faintly, the tightness of the tape around her bones, and her throat was raw, as if she had been trying to breathe but couldn't.

She was afraid to close her eyes, afraid that if she did she would find that she really couldn't open them again. The sense of being trapped was still all around her. Where had she been? She tried to remember more details of the dream, but they were fading as quickly as the chemical smell that had been so strong in the dream. What had it reminded her of? For a moment the oily taste returned to her mouth, but disappeared when she swallowed, trying to place it exactly.

It was only a dream, she reminded herself. A bad dream, definitely, but still only a dream. And the strangest part was that it had come out of nowhere. Before that she'd been having a great dream, one about playing her guitar in front of a crowd at a packed club, her fingers moving over the strings while she sang the lyrics of a song she'd written. She'd been watching the mouths of the people nearest the stage moving along with hers. Then everything had gone black, and the bad dream had begun.

But now it was gone. She was breathing normally

again. Her fingers rested on her chest, and she felt her heart beating. She blinked her eyes, one at a time, testing them to make sure she really could open and close them at will, and then felt ridiculous for even worrying about such a thing. Even as a little girl she had never let nightmares get to her. Dreaming had always been one of her favorite things to do, right up there with submerging herself in the bathtub and looking up through the water while she tried to count all the way to a hundred.

But she had definitely wanted this dream to end. There had been nothing fun about it. It was pure terror, and it bothered her that it had been so difficult to make it end. She had always been able to wake herself up when a dream threatened to become too frightening, and she knew she never wanted to experience what she'd just felt again. Now that she was awake, though, she was back in control.

She looked at the clock next to her bed. It was a little before six. *No sense in going back to sleep*, she told herself. It was almost time to get up anyway. She might as well work on one of her songs until it was time to get ready for school. But as she pulled the covers back and got up to get her notebook, she knew that writing wasn't the only thing that was keeping her from closing her eyes again—part of her was afraid that the dream was waiting for her to come back to it.

She wrote until the night melted away into

dawn and the clear April light crept over her windowsill and spilled onto the floor. Seeing the blueness of the morning sky and the clouds going by like huge, silent sheep drove away the memory of the bad dream. She heard her father walking by her room and going downstairs to get the paper from its place on the front porch, and everything felt right again.

As she showered and dressed for the day, the dream faded from Cooper's memory. After all, she had more important things to occupy her thoughts. It was Monday, and there would be band rehearsal that night at T.J.'s house. Things had been coming together really well ever since she and T.J. had decided to put together a group. She liked the songs they were writing, and for the first time she felt comfortable showing someone else her lyrics.

isobel Bird

join the circle...

Book 1: so mote it be

There's practically nothing about February that Kate likes—the only bright spot is Valentine's Day, and even that looks dreary with no likely prospects in sight. So when a love spell crosses her path, what's a girl to do? Little does Kate know that her impulsive decision to cast a spell will have consequences—both good and bad—far beyond what she'd intended.

0-06-447291-4

Book 3: second sight

As Annie, Cooper, and Kate begin to learn the Craft, a girl in their town goes missing. Cooper has what she thinks are nightmares about it—until it becomes clear that she is having visions about what really happened to the girl. Cooper knows what she must do, but is terrified that it will mean revealing the secret she and her friends have kept until now.

0-06-447293-0